Arcania: Beyond Where the Sidewalk Ends
Book One: If You Are a Dreamer

Royall Agency
9100 Wilshire Blvd., STE333 #109
Beverly Hills, CA 90212

Visit www.royall.agency or call +1 (808) 301-0535 for more information.

This is a work of fiction. The story and illustrations are products of the author's imagination. Names, characters, places, and events are products of the author's imagination or are used fictitiously. Consistent with any literary work, indeed any creative work in any medium, there are myriad sources of inspiration: life experience, creations from other artists, ideas channeled from the chimes of spirits, notions summoned from the swamps of the ether... Regardless, no part of this story— character, person, or place—is intended to represent any person, character, or place occurring or existing, past or present, outside of, or beyond this book. Any resemblance to actual events, locales, characters, or persons living or dead, real or imaginary, is entirely coincidental. Any opinions, thoughts, or actions expressed or implied herein are those of the characters and not the author or anyone else.

ISBN 979-8-9856360-2-4 Hardback
ISBN 979-8-9856360-7-9 Paperback

KDP ISBN 979-8-3906423-8-2 Hardcover

Beyond Where the Sidewalk Ends

The Arcania Series

Written and illustrated by

R.S. Royall

A Cabanga Publication

"Evolution through Imagination"

Author's Note

At the end of the day... if the doorway to reality is hinged on relative perception and fallible memory, do we ever truly know what is real and what is fantasy? The magic and fantastical imaginings of childhood may indeed be real, but as we grow up, our unadulterated creativity is overrun by logic. We yield to more 'reasonable' and socially-acceptable explanations of the mysterious, diminishing the magic of the world and dismissing our creative intuition. Those moments inspiring us to wonder and wander become little more than quaint stories of childhood fantasy, summarily dismissed and archived in the deep places, in oft forgotten files labeled 'musings of an overactive imagination.'

This series is a fictional tale about a boy who has yet to tame or outgrow his overactive imagination. In fact he nourishes it. As a result, he is rewarded with an epic adventure that prepares him for life as a celebrated artist and storyteller.

Although the Arcania story has been written to be entertaining, there are elements of seriousness, contemplation, introspection, and philosophy. Some passages may drift over the heads of younger readers. That's okay. This is intentional, a means of encouraging critical thinking and mindfulness alongside creativity and curiosity.

The reader might also encounter outright nonsense and bizarre silliness seemingly out-of-place or arbitrary to the arc. This too is intentional, for life doesn't always have a clear point, or purpose, or logical flow.

I wish to express my profound gratitude to the following for providing support, input, feedback, and/or editing during the production of this book: Eli Wahler, Laura Kofler, Erin McAuley, Robert Hunter, Dave Tell, Scott Young, and Jordyn Smith. Thank you!

As one might guess, this story is primarily inspired by, and celebrates, the work of Shel Silverstein. It also includes elements from, and is inspired by, my own life experiences, as well as children's books by Dr. Seuss, Antoine de Saint-Exupéry, Joseph Jacobs, Lewis Carroll, J.M. Barrie, A.A. Milne, Maurice Sendak, and Robert Louis Stevenson, to name a few.

In my life, Shel Silverstein's poems and stories have stood out as a rare spice in the dish of children's literature, offering a unique lens through which to view the world, see things from new perspectives.

What Shel gave me through his books, as a youth searching for answers in a difficult world, was profound and priceless. I am not only compelled to give back, I am inspired to create something new.

My intention and hope with the Arcania story is to honor Shel's memory by providing some entertainment for those seeking to trek further down the twisting trails that Shel blazed with his unique poetry, go beyond the point where his work—his sidewalk—ended.

In his book *Every Thing On It*, Silverstein requests that his readers 'writesingtelldraw' something for him after all he's writtensungtolddrawn for them. Well, Mr. Silverstein, this is my 'writesingtelldraw' for you. I hope you like it.

B. Royall

"Imagination is more important than knowledge!"

Far out beyond where the sidewalk ends
Stands a deserted house, attic light all aglow,
Calling dreamers and magic bean make-believers
To the land of flying shoes where the Giving Trees grow.

Where giants roam and mermaids run free.
Where gun-toting lions frighten hunters away.
Where monsters and fat cats wax philosophically,
Where witches fly vacuums and cook food-fighting fray.

Where young girls skip school to devour whole whales,
While peanut butter stick-stuck makes beggars of kings.
Where bears dance, turtles run, and crocodiles spin tales.
Where elephants climb trees and long to fly without wings.

It's a special place to let your imagination run wild.
So run with me and fall up into the blue,
to a world made for silly hearts, both grown-up and child.
The land of wonder called Arcania is waiting for you!

Book One
If You Are a Dreamer

For Lisa,
protector of childhood & encourager of dreams.

Me & Him

Me: **Alright, listen up everybody!** Me and Him, we're gonna tell y'all a wild story...

Book I: Introduction

Him: Um, excuse me. Me?

Me: Yes, Him?

Him: What if they don't want to hear a wild story? What if they don't want to hear any story at all? What if they just want to sit and play guitar and eat blueberry muffins?

Me: Blueberry muffins? What in tarnation are you talkin' about? Eat muffins... Pshhh! Of course they want to hear a story! Who doesn't like a good story?

Him: Well who says it's good? And what if I don't want to tell it?

Me: Oh, you busselfudder! Of course it's a good story! It's about You-Know-Who, and if *you* don't want to tell it, well then you just sit back and be quiet and let *me* tell it!

Him: I-know-who? ...Hang on a sec. You must be talkin' about crazy ol' Sheldon!

Me: The one-and-only! But this story is of an earlier time, about his grand adventure as a boy.

Him: Wait! You mean the story about Sheldon's adventures in Arcania? I love that story! That's where he met—

Me: Whoa! Whoa! Don't give it away!

Him: Oh, right! Sorry. Yes indeedy, that *is* a great tale! I especially enjoy the part where—

Me: Hey now!

Him: Oop. Sorry.

Me: All right then. Apologies, folks. So anyway, Me and Him, we're gonna tell you the tale of a young boy and how he overcame his fear of being a nobody to find his courage, his voice, and become a somebody.

Him: Now, Me will do his best to stay out of your way and just recount the story. Isn't that right, Me?

Book I: Introduction

Me: Wha? Me? You're the one who—

Him: Riiiight, Me??

Me: Ugh. Yes, Him. I'll try to keep quiet. But every once in a while, we may need to chime in here and there to—

Him: Add our own commentary!

Me: See!! You do it too! Sometimes we both get excited and carried away and we just have to—

Him: Jump in!

Me: Exactly! So, if the odd flying comment soars across the page, you'll know it's us, Me and Him.

Him: Yup. So, we'll do our best to let the audience sort out the details, but I hope you can bear with us. You see, folks, Him and Me, we don't always agree.

Me: We don't?

Him: For instance, I like the mountains and Me prefers the sea. He wants to sleep when I want to get up and par-teee!

Me: Oh-kaaay! Thanks for sharing, Him. What's say we just get on with the story?

Him: Well, all right then. Who's gonna start?

Me: Oh, so now you wanna tell it too?

Him: Well, I just thought—

Me: I'm razin' ya! Of course you can tell it with me.

Him: Oh, thanks! You know, sometimes you can be such a sweet—

Me: Now pipe down while I kick this thing off!

Him: Oh... okay, well, I guess that's... Um, where were you... planning to start?

Me: Well, I figured I'd start with the *dream.*

Him: The dream? What dream?

Book I: Introduction

Me: *Theee* dream!

Him: Oh! You mean the one that sets the scene for *everything*? Yeah, that seems like a good place to start I s'pose.

Me: Ya think?

Him: Well, yeah, because, you know, it set the scene for everything and— Ohhhh, you were doing that sarcasm thing again.

Me: Mmm hmm. Are you finished? Can I start?

Him: Sure, go ahead. Take us back to the spring of 1943, Me!

Me: All right then. It was a dark and stormy night...

Him: Wait, what?!

Me: Just kidding.

Him: Oh! Ha ha! That was funny. At first I thought you were—

Me: Actually it *was* a dark and stormy night.

Him: Well, yeah, but not when the dream *starts*.

Me: Nope, not when it starts. So? We ready to do this thing now? This time for real?

Him: Wait, for *reeeaaal* for real?

Me: Well... I guess *that* remains to be seen...

True Story

Her hair flowed wildly as she bolted through the sultry desert, beads of sweat pouring over her flexing muscles, giving her coat a brilliant sheen that glistened like wildfire in the red sunrise...

Book I: Prologue

Like the rooster tail of a racing speedboat, sand and dirt flew high in her wake, while outlaw bullets cut fiercely through the crisp air, licking the ten-gallon hat and snakeskin boots of her spirited, young rider.

"I'm 'unna getcha!" warned the miniature lead missiles, flashing sinister grins as they rocketed past at a thousand miles an hour.

The boy suddenly felt a sharp stab in his side like the sting of a devil scorpion. He looked down in a panic to see a bullet slug smiling victoriously up at him.

"Gotcha!"

The boy frowned at the blood-red river discharging from his side like the Rio Grande from the Rockies. Somewhere high above in the blood-red morning sky, an eagle screeched out a warning:

"You'd best find shelter, boy—and fast."

A cave in the distance answered the call.

"Quick, boy, over here!"

The cowboy yanked the reins, eliciting a ferocious grunt from his horse as she deftly changed course like a swallow in flight. A mad dash for safety sent both horse and rider sailing through the entrance of the cave and they disappeared into darkness.

Safe from the outlaws—for now—the young cowboy dismounted, grimacing as he swung his leg over the horse and slid to the ground, collapsing on the cave floor. After catching his breath, he stood slowly and examined the wound, dread turning to relief upon realizing it was a clean shot straight through the back and out the front. A graze really, no major harm done.

"Would ya look at that!" he smirked at the liquid adventure leaking from his side. *I've survived worse!* He thought, tearing his shirt sleeves into strips for bandages and wrapping the wound. Once the worst of it was cleaned and dressed, he filled his hat with not quite ten gallons of water from the cold, dark crick running through the cavern. "Here y'are, ol' Sundance girl. Drink up."

Book I: Prologue

The horse lapped the refreshing water and shook her head as if trying to jettison the tension of the chase, then wandered in search of anything resembling grass. Exhausted, the boy lay down and rested his head on a rock, feeling about as cozy as a catfish on a cactus. The ramblin' desperado was accustomed to rough country, however, and quickly settled in.

But just as the old Sandman drew near—knapsack full of golden dreams, wonder dust trickling through outstretched fists—a terrifying noise filled the cave. The low growl of a wildcat echoed like rolling thunder through the darkness, frightening the sand genie away and startling the boy awake. He quickly jumped up and whistled for his trusty steed, nervously scanning the surroundings.

Is that a figure moving silently in the shadows or just my eyes playing tricks? He carefully unsnapped the leather strap holding his buck knife to his belt. *Are those yellow eyes of doom staring back at me from the deep?* He slowly withdrew the blade. *Or is my darned imagination prospecting for gold nuggets at the most inopportune time??*

Before he could discern whether he was being stalked, in a raging flash Sundance sprang from the shadows and scooped him up, narrowly escaping a large paw reaching out from the abyss; the cougar taking aim at the alluring red flag that was the boy's blood-stained shirt.

Bolting toward the cave opening, Sundance lowered her head and narrowed her eyes, readying herself for another exciting chase. In the very next instant, however, her eyes widened and her head jerked back, as her rider—who couldn't seem to make up his mind—yanked hard on the reins, locking the horse's forelegs. They skidded to a halt just before daylight gave them away to the gun-slinging outlaws; rowdy taunts tumbling into the cave like an avalanche of boulders roaring down the canyon. The enemy was closing in.

The boy knew they couldn't risk being out in the open, but he also didn't much care to become morning brunch for a malicious mountain lion. Out of options, he spun Sundance around to face the ferocious glowing eyes floating in the black depth.

Book I: Prologue

"N-now... s-see here, c-c-cat! I know I p-probably look m-mighty tasty to you, b-b-but the truth is I'm rotten to the c-c-core! Infested with p-parasites and scrawny all the way 'round. Nothin' but skin and b-b-bones really."

The lion emerged into the dim light, revealing her fearsome size, not less than half as big as Sundance, maybe more. "B-but, just outside this here c-c-cave," the boy continued in terror, "are three uh the most scrumptious and p-plump lunches you c-c-could ask for. An all-you-can-eat buffet, r-r-really."

Staring back with ravenous eyes, the cat stalked the horse and rider, whispering in a confident growl, "If you want me to *not* eat you, you're going to have to *really* sell it, compadre!"

"All right. Okay. I hear ya," the cowboy nodded slowly, careful not to make any sudden moves. "Just..." he gulped, "...consider this: I think the big one out there got hold of your b-brother last w-week. Them's are hunters, they are. Mean ol' gun-lovin', animal-hatin' killers. They were comin' after me 'cause I was tryin' tuh save a helpless little turtle. Poor guy was just out for his mornin' jog in the cool uh the desert and—"

"WHAT DO I CARE ABOUT TURTLES!" the wildcat snapped, drawing ever nearer, a stray glint of sunlight illuminating her teeth shining clear as daggers at high noon. She wasn't buying his story.

"You gotta believe me! Go see fer yourself. The big one's wearing catskin chaps right now! Skin that looks a lot like yours, I reckon."

The puma grimaced and crouched low, readying to pounce. The boy closed his eyes and prepared for the end. The cat leaped! But instead of tackling the boy, she soared clean over his head, flying out of the cave with a roar that sounded a lot like, "For lunch! ...and *VENGEANCE!*"

Both the boy and his trusty steed stood frozen, gulping sighs of relief and listening with profound satisfaction to the taunts of angry men turn to cries of scared boys as the lion chased the outlaws into the desert sunrise.

Book I: Prologue

Feeling much safer, the cowboy dismounted his steed with the pride of having outwitted his enemies; and as Sundance trotted off once more in search of food, he laid his head back down on his comfy rock, tilted his heavy hat over his heavy eyes, and quickly fell into a deep sleep.

o   o   o   o   o   o   o

While the boy slept soundly, however, another adversary moved in the darkness. As luck would have it—bad luck—the cowboy had settled in a cave that happened to be an underground passage to the not-too-distant sea; and where there be sea, there be pirates!

With a painful jolt, the boy awoke to find himself no longer in the desert but on a beach, tied up in pirate rope, hanging from a pirate spit, roasting over a pirate fire. With wide eyes he tried to call out, to scream, to whistle for Sundance, but it was no use; his mouth had been stuffed and bound with the fragments of a Jolly Roger. All he could do was rotate, and while rotating, count one, two, three ragged and dingy pirates sitting nearby, watching him spin and struggle.

As the sky spun into view, he spotted an enormous eagle at the top of the roasting pole, looking down at him with glaring eyes.

"I showed you the cave, but you weren't supposed to stay there! And you certainly weren't supposed to fall asleep in there! I'm sorry but there's nothing I can do for you now." The eagle stretched her enormous wings and lifted into the air, fanning the flames as she departed.

Feeling the heat intensify, the boy became desperate for his horse. He had to get out of there! But ol' Sundance was nowhere to be found. *What could have happened to her, my trusty steed and loyal companion?*

"Arrr, this be the last round up fer ye, landlubber!" A raspy, peg-leg-of-a-voice interrupted his thoughts. From behind thick smoke hanging in the air like a curtain, the boy could just make out a figure approaching.

Book I: Prologue

He frantically struggled to free himself but his bonds wouldn't budge. The fire crackling beneath him had helped to cauterize his bullet wound—a grace of sorts — but it was also burning him to a crisp, or so he felt.

He could sense his consciousness departing, trying to escape the pain, when suddenly a tremendous wave crashed over the rocky shore, extinguishing the fire and knocking over the pole to which he'd been tied. The heat immediately subsided as the torrent of saltwater engulfed the fire, snapping the roasting pole and thrashing the boy against the rocky shore like laundry rags in a tub.

As the wave receded and the tumult turned to calm, the boy's spinning vision settled on the captivating figure of a woman standing on the nearby shore. He was astonished to discover that the woman was part fish! From the waist down she bore a shiny fin that flashed multi-colored as she moved gracefully in the sunlight, dancing to the tune of her triumphant rescue. (How the she-fish was *standing*, let alone dancing, is anybody's guess. But there she was in all her glory!)

The drenched pirates scrambled to capture the rare beauty, but she was too cunning, too quick, and too slippery. Dodging the pirates' attacks, she made for the boy on the spit. Before any of the scalawags knew it, the mermaid had freed the boy and was dragging him toward the sea, no doubt with the intent of stashing her prize away in Davy Jones' Locker.

In a strange fish language that somehow the boy could understand, she spoke, "Hold onto your hat!" as she plunged into the chilly water, grasping tightly to her treasure. Down, down to the deep she swam, the boy struggling all the while in her scaly grasp, knowing full well he would drown if he could not break free. He tugged and tussled in her tangled tentacles. (Does a mermaid have tentacles?) He squirmed and shook, fidgeted and fought, pushed and pinched until finally, she'd had enough.

She stopped swimming and looked at her ungrateful captive. "Whatever is the matter, my love?" Didn't he realize she had just saved his life?

Shaking his head wildly and pointing to his mouth he signaled, "I can't breathe, you maniacal mermaid!"

Book I: Prologue

The fish-lady instantly realized her mistake. This one was not fish! This one was human! And a young one at that, not unlike herself. With terrific haste, she raced the boy back to the surface.

They blasted out of the water and the boy chomped at the air, gulping for more and more as if tasting its splendor for the first time. He instantly coughed up a heap of water (probably enough to fill his long-gone ten-gallon hat) along with something that looked like a small octopus.

"Oh, you're so wild and brave and handsome," the mermaid praised. "I thought you were a mermaid like me, captured by those nasty mermaid-snatching pirates! But you're a human! With legs! How marvelous! Oh, won't you please marry me?"

"WHAT!?" he choked. And yet, given the way things had been going, he somehow expected this sort of nonsense. Seeing her desperate affection, he conceded. "Uh, okay, look, I'll make you a deal. If you swim me to shore so I can rest a while, I'll agree to marry you."

The mermaid lit up and rushed him to the beach. Relieved and exhausted, the boy rolled in the sand, grateful to be back on dry land. "Listen," he said, standing up and brushing the sand from his clothes. "I have to go gather my things. I will be back for you on Wednesday and we can get married then. How 'bout that?"

The mermaid smiled and nodded excitedly.

Wasting no time, the boy ran into the jungle, never to return. No sooner had he left the beach, however, than he found himself knee-deep in a swamp of quicksand.

"Why does this keep happening?!"

Trying not to panic, he reached for a nearby vine, which mysteriously dodged his grasp and hissed violently, "I beg your pardon!"

The vine, which had been slithering happily across the muck, minding its own business, had no intention of being man-handled by a meandering cowboy, a wannabe mermaid, or a jungle tourist; not least of all a combination of the three.

Book I: Prologue

"Oh! Gosh, I'm terribly sorry! I didn't realize you were... That is, I thought you were a tree vine."

"Well, I never!" replied the snake. "As long as we're judging appearances, I'd say you were a hippopotamus's buttocks!" The snooty serpent began to slink away across the mire, beyond satisfied with her retort.

"No, wait! Please don't go. Help me! Help me and I'll... I'll do anything!" The boy was up to his chest and sinking fast.

"Oh, all right. Keep your pants on, if they haven't come off already. Grab hold of something and hang on." The snake offered the boy a middle section of her long, thick torso. Without hesitation, the boy snatched a fistful, and like a small tugboat pulling a freighter, the reluctant reptile slogged the soggy sap slowly through the slop.

The boy felt a tinge apprehensive about being dragged away from the beach, deeper into the thick, forbidding jungle, but he let it slide. When they finally reached solid ground, he looked up to see a massive silhouette towering over him. Since the figure was not a mermaid, a scurvy pirate, or a rascally outlaw cowboy, the boy was relieved... momentarily.

"Here you are. Dinner is served," concluded the snake, wriggling free of the boy's grip and slinking into the bushes.

"Oh, thank you, snake! I *am* starving. How did you know?" The boy's words overflowed with gratitude and anticipation of a long-overdue meal.

"I wasn't talking to you!" was the last thing the boy heard as the reptile slipped into the underbrush and disappeared.

"Wait, what!?" The boy froze as the snake's loaded words sank in (much like the outlaw bullet). Before the snake could reply—not that she was going to—a beefy, calloused hand swiftly grabbed hold of the boy's collar and yanked him from the swamp. In a blur, the boy flew into the air then was quickly hog-tied to a makeshift platform of wooden poles resting atop the shoulders of two stout men.

"Wait a minute! Where are you taking me? Let me go!"

Book I: Prologue

The human caravan said nothing as they marched their captive through the jungle, eventually emerging into a clearing lined with mud-and-thatch huts. Dividing the clearing was a long line of people, apparently waiting for something important.

What could it be? The boy grew anxious and squirmy, strapped to his bamboo bed as the men carried him to the front of the line. Perhaps it was the line for a jungle amusement park. *How fun!* he thought, almost out loud. But before any amusement could be had, the men tore away the boy's bonds and dumped him, face down, onto the forest floor. Annoyed at being discarded like a bad poker hand, he wiped the mud from his face and looked up to see a giant beast of a man sitting atop a large throne of roots, rocks, branches, and bones, all held together by vines... or possibly snakes!

No! It can't be!

Towering over the trembling youth, wearing robes of jaguar fur adorned with what must have been a thousand pounds of brilliantly-colored parrot plumage, sat the notorious, dreaded cannibal chief of the jungle, the infamous Roast-Em-Up Roy! Everyone knew the stories of Roaster Roy, even this young cowboy from the desert.

The cannibal's reputation, the boy knew beyond doubt, meant that this would be the end for sure. But just as the chief reached to pluck his meal from the ground with an enormous fork, mouth salivating something awful, out from the crowd came a cry of protest, "MEEE FIRRRSSST!" The command rang through the forest like a war siren as an impossibly loud, impossibly impatient young girl pushed and shoved her way to the front of the line of people waiting to be seen by—or eaten by—Chief Roy.

Roy's fork paused as he glanced up with a prodigious frown, searching for the imbecile who would dare disturb his meal.

"Nobody, and I mean NOBODY makes Melinda wait in line! If there's something going on, something to do, something to see, *I'll* be the first! You hear me?! First to do it; first to see it; first to—"

Melinda's rant stopped abruptly as she reached the head of the line and realized with horror what awaited her and the rest of the queue.

Immediately, Roy's guards seized the girl, much to her astonishment and dismay.

"Don't worry, darling, you're next!" Roy boomed a nefarious roaring laugh as he made to resume plucking the trembling cowboy from the ground. In that very instant, however, a giant eagle swooped down, grabbed hold of the boy-who-would-be-dinner, and jetted off, soaring clean over the forest canopy.

Stunned, Roy's fork froze in midair, as his warrior-guards sprang into action, flinging spears skyward, attempting to retrieve the airborne hors d'oeuvre. The eagle easily dodged the spears and arrows, spinning deftly in upward spirals, flying high with her captive. Once again the boy was saved from disaster.

Overjoyed, he called to the eagle, "Oh, thank goodness! You have no idea how much I—AAAAAAHHH!!"

Without warning, the bird opened her talons, sending her catch hurtling back to Earth. The boy twisted and turned, trying to get a look at the ground, hoping to find a hot air balloon, another fluffy bird, a flying carpet... something, anything that might catch him or provide a soft landing. But there was nothing. Nothing but water. Lots and lots of water as far as the eye could see in every direction. No land in sight whatsoever.

He thought momentarily that perhaps the water might provide a soft landing, but his hopes faded as he realized there could be no mermaid or any other creature waiting to save him this time. For the sea, he concluded with resolute terror, was rolling in a boil like a steaming-mad kettle of tea left on the stove far too long.

So this is my destiny, he lamented. *I am to be boiled like carrots in a stew!*

The eagle answered with a resounding screech, echoing through the sky, affirming the boy's stew-fate before disappearing into the wild blue yonder.

When the boy finally splashed down, he could feel the water only for an instant, like solid concrete—unbearably hot, solid concrete. As if an egg cracked open on the scorching asphalt of Chicago in August, the boy sizzled, until the pain, lasting but an instant before everything went numb, became a distant memory.

The last thing he felt as his eyes closed their final curtain was the sensation that his entire being was evaporating to steam, floating up to the atmosphere, forming a dense, dark cloud, the precursor to a tremendous rainstorm.

Illuminate

The torrent of rain that hammered the boy's roof and pelted his window throughout the long night, washing away old and preparing for new, as rainstorms do, eventually gave way to clear, calm skies filled with the faint whisper of a most unusual sunrise.

In that freshly cleansed morning, a rogue strand of sunlight appeared against the pale backdrop of a late spring dawn, like a warrior perched atop a distant hill, surveying her battlefield before war. This curious beam shone brightly from well beyond the far-away horizon, a cosmic searchlight scouring the heavens for a wayward traveler, a lost friend alone somewhere out in the world. As the playful spotlight danced and twirled across the landscape — searching, searching — a familiar thing caught her attention and she settled excitedly on a particular house, an apartment rather. There, in some modest building nestled in a nook just outside of downtown Chicago, a young boy struggled through corrupted dreams of cowboy outlaws and cannibal pirates.

On a singular window of this small apartment, the light paused, intensifying her radiance to cut a clear path through the morning fog, announcing a brand-new day, and along with it, destiny. The focused beam, dedicated to her mission of finding her friend, eventually succeeded at penetrating the curtained window of that Chicago apartment. Into the previously darkened room she crept, silently stalking her prey, hovering over the slumbering boy, reveling in her success at finally finding him. Then, playful as always, she smacked him right across the face!

"Take that, you loafing laggard!" she laughed.

The boy flinched, rolled over, and smothered his assaulted mug in his pillow, yanking his blanket over his head. "Go away!" he complained. After all the stress and turmoil throughout the night, he felt thoroughly unprepared for a new day that was sure to bring its own challenges.

But the tenacious luminescence did not go away. Undaunted, she deftly navigated the folds in the pillow and blanket. She hadn't come this far to be thwarted by feeble linens. There, at the precipice of his senses, she joined forces with the morning clamor of the house already seeping through the pillow fluff like soldiers in a snowstorm.

Wishing he could clamp his ears shut as he could his eyes, the boy growled at the intrusion. It was no use. Together, the warriors of light and sound fought a successful campaign, forcing the surrender of his slumber.

He sat up abruptly, defiantly, as the droning of his parents arguing with his aunt about some grownup nonsense came crashing into his room, a victory parade for the morning light's hard-fought battle. In the background, a radio scratched updates about a very different battle. The war overseas was escalating according to the woeful morning report, dragging the economy (whatever that was) "down into the muddy trenches along with it," reported the hollow voice from the talking telegram.

"Ugh. Grown-ups!" The boy rubbed the sleep from his eyes. Blinking in rapid squints, he attempted to let the intrusive dawn in only a little at a time. Upon seeing him waking, however, the full force of the morning glow crashed through the slit in his curtains like an anxious puppy, somehow looking, so the boy thought, as if it were smiling.

"It's not funny! I'm tired! And what's all this racket?!" The boy shifted his squinty scowl from the window to his bedroom door, half expecting a parade to burst through at any moment. He frowned at the sound of his sister running down the hall, laughing with their cousin and yelling about the bathroom or boys or bows in their braids. Oh, his spoiled kid sister, who always hogged the attention and only had one task; just one, single, itsy-bitsy chore.

"Take out the garbage. That's all we ask," their parents would remind her every single day. But no! She refused, apparently above soiling her hands with manual labor. And she got away with it too! She got away with loads of stuff, like skipping school by feigning sick.

"I've got a sore throat... I think I swallowed a tree! I've a headache like a house fell on me! ... Purple spots all over my belly ... Swollen feet that make me walk silly ... No, school's just not gonna work for me today ... unfortunately."

And would you believe that nonsense worked!? She could get away with anything!

But not me! He fell back on his pillow and yanked the covers over his head, a last-ditch effort to go back to the land of dreams; even cursed ones so long as it was sleep.

Send in the reserves!

A blitzkrieg of car horns and pedestrian sounds announcing the day's commerce marched into his room from the streets below, joining the fight to get the lazy kid out of bed. A harangue descended over him like a storm of sewing pins, pricking his senses, making him cringe.

"Is every day National Noise Day around here?!" he barked from under the covers. He almost thought he heard a giggle in response, as if the annoying morning light were enjoying the pandemonium. "Hey, everyone, pick a noisemaker!" He tossed the blankets off his head. "Pots and pans, clapping hands, stomping shoes, the latest news..." It was all just noise, noise, noise! What a miserable start to—

Wait! Wait just a minute! "I'm alive!" he exclaimed, quickly sitting up and taking stock of his state. "No bleeding from bullet holes or broiling over barbecues!"

The light smiled.

"No being sunk by she-fish or served up for supper!"

The light nodded.

"No boiling alive in a giant lake, for heaven's sake!"

The light smiled and nodded.

Feeling renewed, he discarded his quilted blanket—along with his reservations—sending stitched cheetahs, giraffes, rhinos, and lions tumbling in all directions. Stretching a mighty stretch and yawning a mighty yawn, he looked around, surveying his kingdom. "Gee-whiz! Whosever room this is ought to be ashamed. What a mess!" he chuckled. Then, without further thought, he jumped up and walked right out of his messy room... and immediately walked back in. In a house full of people, sometimes people you don't know, it's advisable to get dressed *before* leaving your room.

The boy snatched whatever clothes were within reach and shoved them on whichever body parts put up the least resistance, looking like a magician trying to escape a straitjacket. "What's the deal?!" It was as if his clothes belonged to someone else, or he were an entirely different person than yesterday.

Twisting and squirming—eliciting more giggles from the intruding sunbeam—the boy charged down the hall toward the bathroom, but not before closing his bedroom door with a smirk, leaving the mischievous light to find its own way out.

At the miniature sink in the cramped bathroom, the boy splashed cold water on his face and paused at the reflection in the silver-clouded mirror, making sure he was still the same person he was when he went to sleep the night before. "Hmm. Unclear."

His reflection squinted back with gritted teeth. "This bathroom ain't big enough fer the both of us!" the boy in the mirror growled.

He chuckled to himself and ran a river of cool water over his scalp. Pulling his hair away from his face, he slicked his mane back, taking advantage of its own natural, oily residue. Despite the hair which seemed to grow enthusiastically everywhere else on his body, he could swear the hair on his head was already thinning. It wasn't. In fact, after drying out, his mane tended to puff up in thick waves, curls encircling his head like a crown of smoky thoughts emanating from the fire of his imagination.

This was an odd morning indeed. The mirror must've been in cahoots with the mischievous light. That, or he wasn't fully awake. For surrounding his reflection were fanciful characters and scenes from his nightmarish dream. He glanced over his shoulder to make sure there wasn't *actually* a dragon looming behind him then splashed more water on his face to dissolve the illusions.

After nearly drowning himself, he looked up at the face staring back at him. *Good grief.* The unruly locks, winged ears, and gap in his front teeth did little to boost his confidence. "Quite the ladies' man, aren't you?" he jested with a mournful shake of his oversized head.

He fumbled with one hand, adjusting his uncooperative shirt and some uncooperative hairs on his head, and with the other, did his best to brush his teeth sans toothpaste. A shortage of toothpaste wasn't the worst thing he'd experienced as a result of the current economic recession but it sure didn't help freshen up the morning routine.

Placing his toothbrush back in the cup next to the sink, he winked at his compadre in the mirror and continued into the hall, slinking past the adults blabbering away in the living room. He imagined gluing their mouths shut with some extra-sticky peanut butter—temporarily of course—just to get a moment's peace from all of the adult-speak jibber-jabber, those never-ending dos and don'ts, woeful criticizing and complaining.

"He mustn't..."

"She shouldn't..."

"They'll never..."

Why are adults so grumpy all the time? he shook his head. *So negative and doubting of—*

"Oh, that's impossible!"

"...everything," he concluded, quietly shuffling into the kitchen, being particularly careful to avoid being seen by his father. If ever there were someone who needed his heart softened and mouth glued shut, it was his dear old, dissatisfied, disappointed, disapproving dad. If only his old man would stop complaining, stop barking orders long enough to see, to really see, and in seeing to truly appreciate, the miracle of his children. *Maybe someday.*

The boy snatched his book bag from the hall tree and squeezed on his worn-out leather shoes, so old they looked as though they could walk (or fly) away without any feet in them. As he drifted through the kitchen, he swiped from the counter someone's toasted bread, conveniently adorned with a generous spread of peanut butter. *Probably Dad's,* he figured. *Hopefully Dad's!* he smirked.

His father loved peanut butter sandwiches above all else it seemed at times. The old monarch hoarded peanut butter like pirate treasure, sneaking sandwiches when he thought no one was looking, even at suppertime when everyone else was forcing down small trees of broccoli. *Not fair!* he thought. He loved peanut butter too. *Oh, glorious peanut butter!* he reveled as he sunk his teeth into the toast, made all the more delicious by the notion of stealing it from under the nose of his pops.

"Thank you!" he whispered in the direction of his father still grumbling away in the next room, wholly unaware that his royal coffers were being robbed. With his scrumptiously sticky treasure in hand, the boy slipped, unnoticed and unaccounted for—as usual—quietly out into the world.

Everything On It

The young peanut butter thief had been walking himself to school for nearly three years, during which time he'd carved a route that passed through the old, abandoned buildings separating Palmer Avenue and Logan Square...

On days with time to spare, he would pause and riffle through the dirt and rubble, looking for interesting treasure, typically finding naught but common items: rusted nails, old medicine bottles, unidentifiable scraps of leather or tin...

On that particular day, however, as he kicked through mounds of dirt and detritus—the playful morning light following him around not unlike his pesky kid sister—he happened to come across an odd-looking piece of jewelry.

"Hey! Look at this!" the light shifted, illuminating the ground as if spotlighting an actor on stage. A shard of something beneath the surface was struggling to respond to the cue. This actor was old, tired, perhaps no longer worthy of an audience. Regardless, the boy was intrigued. Bending down, he pushed his stubby fingers through the dirt, gravel, rubbish, and ash, helping the reluctant remnant into the limelight once more.

"Come on now," he encouraged, exhuming the shard from its tomb. "Perform for me." He spat on the piece and scrubbed away the dirt, revealing what appeared to be a tooth from a prehistoric saber cat or a small dinosaur, perhaps a tiny tusk from a tiny elephant.

The base of the tooth was wrapped with copper wire affixing it to a thoroughly rusted necklace. He spat on it again, rubbing away more grime and examining it closely, turning it over and over in his palm until it came clean, revealing its secrets. He squinted at what looked like the word, 'IF' stamped into the copper. He had never seen anything like it, and yet, something about it felt unmistakably familiar. Getting to the bottom of why that might be, and figuring out what this tooth thing was exactly, was going to require an expert. Luckily, he knew just the person.

○ ○ ○ ○ ○ ○ ○

Because his was the only food cart open at such an early hour for nearly four blocks in any direction, Hector's Hot Dogs was always crowded with the morning rush. Fortunately for the boy, Hector had a soft spot for the adventurous youth and always kept a warm dog ready should the youngster pass by on his way to school.

"Here you go, son, one dog dragged through the garden, just as you like it," Hector would say, handing over a hot dog piled high with just about every topping from his cart. Although that was not 'just how he liked it,' the kid would politely smile and accept the hot mess in exchange for whatever he happened to find in the rubble that morning.

Affectionately known around the neighborhood as Hector the Collector, the hot dog man was a self-proclaimed historian of the Windy City. His food cart was adorned with all the trinkets and trifles brought to him by customers looking to trade treasure for food. Ornaments and decorations hung from every inch of the wooden awning gave his cart the look of a gypsy caravan. Although he was always more than happy to trade one of his dogs for a unique doodad or doohickey, most of the trinkets turned out to be useless junk. Every so often, however, an intriguing puzzle piece of Chicago history would be scavenged up, adding to the décor of the cart and seasoning Hector's days with endless excitement. Judging by what the boy was twirling in his fingers that morning, Hector suspected that it just might turn out to be one of those fortuitous days.

"That's quite remarkable, my friend," Hector hollered as the boy approached. "I don't reckon I've seen the like... not for a very long time and not around these parts, that's for sure." Noting Hector's intrigue, the boy handed him the pendant without hesitation. The hot dog man examined the thing with great interest. "Where did you find it?"

The boy just shrugged, which Hector understood to mean, "somewhere in the dirt."

Pensively stroking his beard and pursing his lips, the Collector grunted, "Hmm. Well, I'm not entirely sure what to make of this..."

Hector was a short, hirsute man with a great, round belly and dark, alluring eyes that told tales of mystery and adventure even when his mouth remained shut, which was almost never. Complimenting his esoteric cart, Hector wore extravagant outfits of cloth that looked to be hand-spun in far-away places, the fringe of the world. A curious collection of chains, chimes, and charms hung from his costume as well as various body parts, giving him the air of a genie freshly popped from a many thousands-year-old bottle.

O O O O O O O

"So you... don't... know what it is?" the boy asked timidly, surprised at Hector's apparent stupefaction. It was uncommon for Hector not to be enthusiastically forthcoming with some creative and entertaining story — usually entirely made up of course — about the treasures people brought him: where the piece originated, its significance in society, purpose in life, etcetera. The kid liked to imagine that Hector, with his elaborate collection of stuff and stories, was a mystical gypsy who had only recently wandered into town from the deserts of Arabia ... or perhaps the moons of Andromeda.

"Oh, no, no. On the contrary, son. I know exactly what this is. But what a crocodile tooth of this ilk is doing in Chicago is beyond even me." The hot dog man let loose one eyebrow and like a wild animal freed from a cage, the thing shimmied up his forehead and perched atop his dome, looking menacingly down at the boy. When a peripheral flash of light caught his eye, the Collector turned and squinted at the low sun stumbling around as if lost in the morning mist. Bits of light trickled through the streets like a search party slowly making its way through a dark forest. "Sure is a curious light over the city this morning." Hector glanced back at the boy and released the second eyebrow which rushed to catch up with its bretheren, the two caterpillar-like things scrutinizing the kid from their lofty post.

The boy looked over Hector's shoulder and scowled at the light. "Curious is one way to put it."

Volleying, the light bounced off a window and flashed the boy square in the eyes, blinding him momentarily. "Ahh!" The boy jerked his head and shielded his face, conceding defeat. Stepping back into the hot dog man's abundant shadow, the boy reached out and gingerly retrieved the pendant.

"Maybe it's leftover from a colony of crocodiles that used to live in Chicago, before the city was here." He twirled the tooth in his fingers, spinning the yarn of his imagination.

"Oh?" queried Hector, his restless brows looking ferociously inquisitive.

"Yeah! They were... farmers, like the old farmers that live outside the city, and they stood up and walked on their hind legs, like us! Except, they were eight feet tall! And they liked to sing and dance!" He flung his arms around and danced about, animating his fanciful tale.

Hector laughed loudly and swiftly picked the pendant back from the boy. Bowing to the young storyteller, he stretched the chain into a wide circle and held it out as if presenting a medal. "Now *that* is a good story! You have quite the imagination, Mr. Silvers." Hector placed the tooth-pendant around the neck of his creative friend and gave the boy a wide-eyed stare. Then, stealing another backward glance at the oncoming light, added with a kind, yet mysterious smile, "And likely an intriguing story unfolding around you today. I think you ought to hold onto this one, Shelby. This treasure belongs to you!"

The boy examined the pendant with renewed curiosity, until Hector interrupted, "Now off you go, Sheldon... before you're late!" With a wink and a nod, Hector shoved a hot dog at the boy then shoved him along toward school.

Stumbling onward, the young Sheldon Silvers looked down at the steaming pile of rubbish Hector had placed in his hands, inspiring more 'um...' than 'yum!' It was well-known that the hot dog man dished out the most decorative franks around, no question about that.

For Sheldon, the hot dog was of much less interest than Hector's company, his contagious laughter, and most of all, his wild stories. He and Hector shared many fanciful conversations about the history and culture of Chicago and beyond, conversations about places and happenings both real and, Sheldon's favorite, entirely made up. These exchanges inspired the young imaginator. He took refuge in Hector's fanciful tales, imagining worlds beyond his noisy apartment and school. The hot dog was merely a formality of the exchange. Sheldon had never developed an affinity for meat anyway, especially those franks with everything but the kitchen sink on 'em. Yuck!

"Who puts jelly on a hot dog?!" Sheldon would grumble. Hector loved jams and jellies, possibly more than hot dogs! Why he never opened a brick-and-mortar delicatessen — or, Sheldon mused, *a jelli-catessen* — was a mystery beyond even the boy's imagination. He figured the hot dog stand was just a side gig, a way for Hector to torture the patrons of Logan Square with his odd food combinations. He was, after all, the only street vendor known to put jelly on a hot dog, much to many-a-customer's dismay. The man did what he wanted and that's what made him interesting, especially to Sheldon, who loved to complain, "What's with all the cucumbers and onions? ... Spinach? Really? ... Hot peppers again? ... I think it's against the law to put broccoli on a hot dog!"

Hector would just laugh his hearty laugh and watch the boy, who was raised with a good sense to appreciate whatever he was given, attempt to force down the creative franks so as to take up space in his belly that would otherwise need to be filled by the so-called 'food' served at Charles R. Darwin Elementary School.

A Good Defense

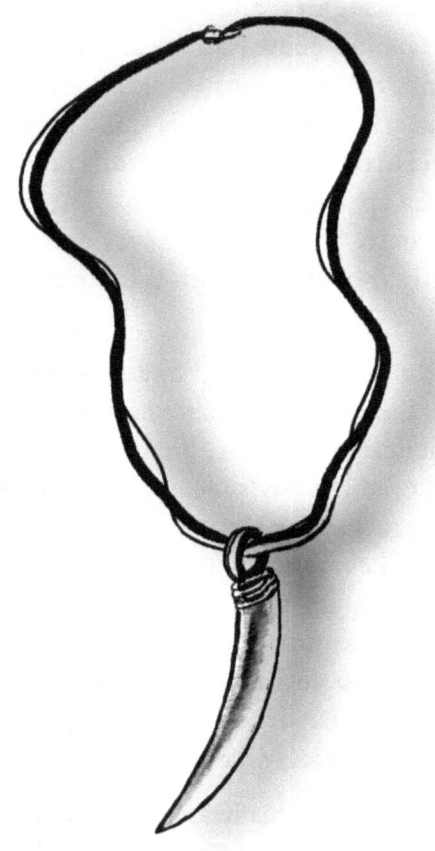

Sheldon didn't have many friends at Darwin Elementary, just two or three acquaintances who would now and again drone out an obligatory, "Hi, Sheldon," in passing. Most of the attention he received was earned through humiliating pranks, practical jokes, and general bullying...

He was a particularly attractive target for notes stuck to his back (or backside), shoelaces tied together while daydreaming in class, or kids playing keep-away with his bookbag. That morning, despite being on campus only a few short minutes, Sheldon had already removed a note stuck to his back that read 'Handle with care,' a postage stamp in the corner of the note indicating someone intended to airmail him to some far-off place—which would be just fine with him.

Get me outta here! he thought, often.

On occasion, he would find some treasure on his way to school and *not* trade it for a messy hot dog (for whatever reason). On those days, upon seeing that Sheldon had found something interesting, a handful of kids would instantly become his best buddies, rubbing elbows against him from all directions, hoping he might give up his fascinating find.

Because Hector insisted Sheldon keep the tooth pendant, and because he now wore it around his neck for all to see, sure enough, a gang began to assemble, asking to see, hold, wear, even keep the treasure. As if by intention, setting the scene for confrontation, a cluster of clouds formed above, mirroring the gathering below and momentarily blocking out the morning sunlight, casting a long, dark shadow over the schoolyard.

"Come on, Sheldon! Don't be stingy!" came a voice from the crowd, and the mob replied in unison, "Yeah!"

The attention Sheldon got from Hector and the attention he received at school could not have been more different. On any other day he might have given in and let the pendant go to whichever kid was the biggest or most aggressive. Out of respect for Hector and the hot dog man's mysterious gesture, Sheldon decided he must hang onto the tooth no matter the cost. He grasped the pendant in a protective fist and pushed his way through the crowd of outstretched groping hands.

"Leave me alone!" he yelled, but of course no one listened. Most kids who Sheldon knew, those at Darwin being no exception, seemed to only speak one language, the language of action, and Sheldon was a boy of intellect not action. (Not yet!)

As the mob grew denser, the pushing and pulling more intense, a voice rang out like the trill of a referee's whistle, halting the rough play. "All right you goons! You heard 'im! Back off!" Sheldon spun around to see Allison Tamaroa, a ruthless force on the Darwin playground, shoving kids aside as she made her way through the mob.

Allison wasn't a bully by any stretch. Quite the opposite in fact. She was known as a bully-fighter, a protector of the innocent and defender of the weak, so to speak. Still, just to be safe, anyone who knew what was good for them steered clear of the Tamaroa Train—a title Allison had earned by plowing over anything and everything in her path—unless they enjoyed knuckle sandwiches for lunch or taking naps face-down in the dirt.

Because Sheldon only encountered Allison when she came to his rescue—which was no more than once a week... twice tops... maybe three times but that's it—and because she never really acknowledged him personally, Sheldon was pretty sure Allison didn't know who he was, other than just another feeble milksop in need of regular saving. Regardless, he was awfully relieved to see her steaming her way toward him, the defense express coming to his rescue once again. With her help, eventually the two of them made it safely through the ornery crowd.

The ordeal sufficiently extinguished, Sheldon turned to thank his knight in shining armor. But before he could get any words out, the train left the station, off to her next stop, leaving Sheldon standing alone, watching his savior walk away. He started daydreaming a little, imagining inviting her to share an ice cream or soda pop. When a shove in his back from a disgruntled mobster reminded him that he'd best move along if he liked his nose in the center of his face, he did just that, carving a beeline for his classroom. Like the young cowboy to his cave, Sheldon quickly sought refuge within the dark halls of Darwin.

Most days at Darwin Elementary, Sheldon passed the entire seven-and-a-half hours in quiet solitude, drawing cartoon sketches on his work papers without anyone, including his teacher, Miss Kelsyan, saying so much as two words to him.

Miss Kelsyan was a tall, slender woman who looked to Sheldon to be at least 150 years old. She wasn't haggard or decrepit by any means. In fact, Sheldon thought she was rather fetching for her exceptional age, with a refined, almost royal air about her. Her manner of speech, dress, and general disposition made Sheldon suspicious that she might secretly be an immortal queen from an age long past. For this mystique, Sheldon enjoyed Miss Kelsyan. He made sure not to mistake his regard for her as any sort of friendship, however, as she made it clear her classroom was a place of discipline, not a social club.

O   O   O   O   O   O   O

The morning bell called the remaining inmates back to the Kelsyan cell block and Sheldon prepared himself for another long day of confinement. That is, he took out his drawing pad and began to doodle and drift away.

The day's lectures were tuning up to the standard key of dull. So, naturally, while Miss Kelsyan droned on about the Civil War, Sheldon's note papers filled up with sketches of cartoon soldiers fighting with noodles instead of swords. He was not a fan of violence. He was, however, fascinated with the *notion* of war, how so-called civilized people time and again avoided prudent, reasonable negotiations in favor of the worst sort of brutalities.

Miss Kelsyan was clearly not fascinated by violence nor war, and her lack of enthusiasm shone brilliantly through her soporific lectures, which were, incidentally, complimented by her drab outfits: blends of dark and light greys, not unlike like the Confederacy itself... or the cloudy skies hanging in perpetuity over Chicago.

While the kids at Darwin maintained the joke that she came from the black and white era before color was invented, Sheldon was pretty sure that Miss Kelsyan—along with many, possibly most, people in Chicago—dressed to match a monochromatic existence devoid of the brilliant colors found in the more exciting places of the world.

In Chicago, with the exception of Hector's wild hot dogs, most things seemed dull and colorless, flavorless meat and potatoes. Maybe that's the reason he spent so much time at Hector's stand: it was full of colorful story and spice. Maybe that's the reason why he spent so much time drawing cartoons: he was trying to animate an otherwise woefully dreary existence.

o o o o o o o

The school day dragged on with Miss Kelsyan's lecture on U.S. history diving deep into famous naval battles; and there sat the incarcerated Sheldon, his desk an iron weight chained to his soul! Sympathetic to his plight, his imagination threw him a lifeline. He eagerly grabbed hold and instantly felt himself pulled away to distant lands.

He fantasized about being on an island, wandering through tropical jungles, surrounded by plants and animals painted every color of the rainbow. He imagined the expeditions undertaken by famous explorers like Livingstone, Hemingway, Roosevelt... His mind trekked across a wondrous expanse of wilderness, danger and excitement dripping from the adventures like too much icing on too hot a cinnamon roll... His thoughts shifted to his father's bakery on N. Western Avenue and the exotic images disappeared behind the steam of a tropical sun, or an overworked oven... Hunger crept up on him like a hunter and he began salivating for rolls of dough... and unchained freedom.

He would invariably conclude that, like his old man's famous cinnamon rolls, the hunting safari stories were too rich for his taste. Nauseatingly so. The trophy killing of creatures like the noble rhinoceros, the regal lion, and his favorite, the majestic elephant, was utterly distasteful to say the least. How much more sporting these epic safaris would be, he mused, if the animals could fight back with some modern technology of their own. Or what if the animals were mutated in some way? He chuckled at the thought of a giraffe with two heads and six legs that could shoot flaming bananas out of its nostrils.

"Hehe!"

Oops! An audible giggle! That was as likely to blip on the Kelsyan radar as an overweight, lazy LaPerm is likely to nap on a lap (which is an absolute certainty).

Sure enough, the student sitting at the desk in front of him—one of Kelsyan's informants no doubt—glanced back with curiosity that quickly transitioned to disapproval when she realized Sheldon was goofing off... again.

He shook his head to recall his attention to the math lesson lest he be sent to the brig. One more slip-up like that and he could expect a torpedo from the Kelsyan battleship, sinking his cruiser to the deep. Like a diving submarine, he slunk in his chair and lowered his head, trying to make himself invisible. The new posture set his eyes level with his coursework and he noticed something that surely would not please the Kelsyan commander who always demanded tidy work. Staring back at him, holding his notes hostage, was the sketch of a lion brandishing a double-barreled shotgun, the words "Friendly greetings from Africa" written above it. He added "Shoot Kodachrome only, or else!" and turned the page just as Miss Kelsyan wandered by, conducting her periodic inspection of her troops.

Imagination Unchained

"Kelsyan... Kel-see-in... keel-sea-in..."

Drop the keel in the sea! came the command from the captain...
Sheldon's attention wandered yet again, inspired by another messy page of
lecture notes woven between random doodlings...

His thoughts drifted like a lonely boat untethered by a careless sailor, coerced to sea by a mischievous tide. Once in open waters, his mind sailed through the classroom window, up into the sky. Recalling Kelsyan's Civil War lecture, the distant clouds transformed into clipper ships with large keels stabbing deep into a tumultuous sea of vapor, swirling on cumulonimbus currents. The Navy's warships had gone airborne with the North hammering the South in a barrage of watermelon cannonballs and spaghetti grapeshot. Captains were ordering regiments of fried fish-sticks into the fray of battle with carrot bayonets on the ends of asparagus stalk rifles... The hot dog with everything on it was wearing off.

"Is it lunchtime yet?" Sheldon's tummy rumbled.

The bell for morning break rang a definitive, "Nope," startling Sheldon from his daydream. He reluctantly stood up and prepared to exit the classroom, grumbling in dismay over the daily playground puerility. *What is recess but an opportunity to flaunt one's popularity through equal measures of social intimidation and athletic prowess?* he lamented. Though coordinated enough to play sports, he preferred instead to play at being sophisticated, avoiding playground games with, "It's my innate aversion to conformity which prevents me from participating." He did, however, get a kick out of watching his peers try to sort out how to respond to that excuse.

Truth was, his lack of participation had more to do with low self-confidence, difficulty asserting himself, and a preoccupation with life beyond school, a sort of big-picture thinking not all that common for kids his age—which wasn't winning him any popularity contests. In fact, the only person possibly less popular might have been the bear-sized dancing boy, Donald Kushvatsky. Whether walking to and from class in the halls or passing time on the playground—really anytime he wasn't being forced to sit still at his desk—Donald was dancing.

Sheldon imagined Donald came from a long line of Slavic ballet dancers and that he'd been told to practice nonstop, or else! To most students, Donald the dancer was simply amusing, but for Sheldon, Donald was an invaluable asset because his dancing took the spotlight off Shel, which worked perfectly because Donald was virtually immune to bullies.

Unlike Sheldon who required the protection of Allison, Donald was big, perhaps the biggest kid in school—a trait which had earned him the nickname The Bear. He kept to himself mostly and seemed friendly enough. Still, even the toughest hooligans kept their distance, not wanting to poke The Bear... and get mauled as a result.

Beyond his invincibility, Sheldon respected Donald for his devil-may-care attitude. The Bear danced whenever and wherever he wanted, pirouetting above adolescent social pressures, setting his sights instead, like Sheldon, on life after Darwin.

It wasn't just the idea of life beyond school that preoccupied Sheldon, he was also obsessed with life beyond his tiny, noisy apartment, life beyond his father's bakery, life beyond Chicago. Even at the age of twelve (twelve years, eight months to be exact), he was already a self-described visionary—though most of his peers used the term 'dreamer' if they were being nice, and they didn't mean the sort of dreamer who would invent the next great novelty. They saw Sheldon as a space-case who provided odd commentary and exhibited odd mannerisms. So it went that Sheldon was consistently ignored by the popular groups and the pretty girls and the team captains looking to pick their players, but not by the bullies looking to tag their targets.

After the attention received on the playground before school that day, Sheldon was convinced he would not return from recess with his pendant. Thus, he did his best to keep a low profile, circumnavigating the schoolyard, putting as much distance as possible between him and everyone else. Miraculously, he was able to pass the entire break without attracting any unwanted attention, no doubt thanks to the residue of Allison Tamaroa lingering in the air around him like a swarm of killer bees. *More like perfume*, Sheldon grinned, convinced that he could still smell her scent, a delusion that helped calm his nerves.

Lost in a daydream about the impressive Allison, Sheldon wandered, as if under a spell, onto the school baseball diamond, right in the middle of a ball game... and *WHAP!*

The next thing he knew, Shel was sitting in the silent solitude of the school nurse's office, blood trickling down his face from saturated tissues stuffed up his nose. Apparently, as the nurses explained, Randy Ickle, who, after The Bear was the second largest kid in school, and who always wore extra large, extra heavy—and perpetually untied—military issue combat boots, lost his shoe during a game of kick baseball after an overly enthusiastic 'swing' sent the boot soaring high into the infield sky. As luck would have it—bad luck—Sheldon caught the boot... with his face... just as Randy slid into second.

Obeying both the school nurses, Sheldon pinched his nose and held his head back to control the bleeding. There he sat in the cold, sterile room, head and face throbbing, when the school bell heralded a stampede of wound-up kids yelling and stomping their way back to class like wild buffalo. He sighed and loosened his grip, letting the blood flow, beyond content to spend the rest of the day right there in peace and quiet.

"Do I hap do go mack do glass?" he wheezed through a nose full of tissue, trying to sound as miserable as possible. "I reary don't veel well." The two nurses, who only used words when absolutely necessary, silently nodded their heads in unison like Siamese cats tracking a bouncing ball.

For reasons known only to a winter orchid, Darwin Elementary had two nurses who filled the one role of school medic, two dutiful twin sisters, always working together, side by side, never one without the other, as if they would perish if separated. Because Sheldon spent a good deal of time in the infirmary, he had developed—or so he imagined—a special rapport with the twins. He concluded that they were possibly the nicest people in the entire school on account of their attentive care. It was hard to tell what they were really like, however, as neither of them said much at all, which made them even more likable to Sheldon. The twins worked swiftly and effectively, letting their practically-impeccable healing skills do the talking.

When Sheldon requested to stay in the infirmary, he expected the sweet ladies to hand him a blanket and a cup of tea, perhaps a biscuit or cookie, and conclude with silent gestures to make himself comfortable. Instead, the first pointed toward the door and with a gentle smile said,

"Cafeteria." The second, also behind a soft smile, concluded with, "Ice." And with that, they handed him not a cup of tea nor a blanket, nor even a cookie, but a wad of gauze and a note for his teacher, then summarily escorted him out the door.

Released back into general population, Sheldon wandered the halls, slowly taking the scenic route to the cafeteria, which wasn't scenic at all unless one appreciated the various scratches, dents, and hues of cream on the endless rows of lockers. The windows of Darwin were few and far between, letting only a minimal amount of light in and even less imagination out. Perhaps that was intentional, for keeping students focused. *In other words, tame*, he concluded.

He eventually arrived at the cafeteria as the cooks were preparing their usual mystery slop for lunch. He didn't know the women who worked there as well as he did the nurses, but he was fascinated by them even more. They may have been the sweetest ladies in the world, but based on the food they prepared and the mysterious way they worked behind the counter, Sheldon had no choice but to conclude they were witches, brewing concoctions to suppress the energetic dispositions of the unruly masses; that is, turn the kids into mindless zombies. After all, how could so many spirited children sit still for so many hours day after day?

It's just not natural!

The elderly cooks wore ankle-length, dark grey dresses and large hats that concealed their long hair tied up in messy buns. They never seemed very keen to chat with any of the kids (Sheldon couldn't blame them for that). Instead, they chatted nonstop with one another in a language no one could understand.

Sheldon did not speak any language other than English but he could recognize foreign words from time to time. Family friends from the synagogue, patrons in his father's bakery and around Hector's stand, even some of his family members who still spoke the 'old tongue' allowed him to recognize accents of Russian, German, Yiddish, Polish, French, and Italian. But these ladies spoke something altogether foreign, some language dominated by giggles and cackles.

The lunch ladies laughed nonstop, ignoring the boy in bandages standing silently at the counter, no doubt looking terrifically pitiful. No matter. Sheldon wasn't in any hurry to get back to class. He certainly did not want to disturb the witches for fear they might turn him into a toad. So, there he stood, silently waiting at the lunch counter, long enough for the bleeding to stop, unfortunately.

When one of the women eventually acknowledged him and approached, he began to speak, to explain why he was there and what he needed, but the woman cut him off by tossing a bag of ice loudly onto the counter, only momentarily pausing her cackling chatter to flash a wide grin, revealing a sparse set of crooked, off-color teeth that made Sheldon cringe. How did she know what he wanted?

Because she's a witch!

o o o o o o o

Along the walk back to Kelsyan's classroom, through the desolate and dark hallways, Shel noticed the school's main entryway doors had been left slightly ajar, unusual for the typically locked-down Darwin. Suddenly, a bright beam of light flashed from beyond the threshold, teasing him with unattainable freedom.

"Ah, you're back!" he squinted at the light. "That was very rude, by the way, waking me up this morning the way you did." The light in the door stayed ruefully quiet, dimming slightly, looking apologetic. "Ugh, it's okay," offered Sheldon. "Don't sweat it."

The light perked up, skipping brightly around the room, beckoning him to come and play. Sheldon shook his head. "I can't." *...Still, I suppose a little daydream couldn't hurt.* He squinted at the illuminated crack in the doorway and imagined a small lizard in a dark cave, slipping out through the fissure, recharging its batteries in the glorious sunshine of a wide-open desert. His mind became a wild reptile wandering free in a boundless landscape while his body adhered to the mantra of obedience recited daily within the halls of Darwin: Stand still, be quiet, keep your hands to yourself. Sit, stay, roll over. Good dog.

I wonder when things are going to evolve around here, he thought, often.

The strict discipline seemed so old-fashioned. With a sigh, his reptilian fantasy faded, and he found himself at the entrance to Commander Kelsyan's barracks, hand congealed around the doorknob. Looking back at the school entrance, he watched as the lizard sped off into the desert without him.

"Traitor."

The bag of ice turning his hand into a popsicle gave him a chilling thought and he took his revenge on the turncoat reptile, imagining the warm sunshine suddenly degrading to a white-out blizzard. "Take that!" The freezing lizard in a blizzard was sure to get a snowflake in his gizzard. *So there!* He smiled in triumph. A moment later he felt sorry for his imaginary friend, but what could do? "C'est la guerre!" He shrugged, turning back toward the classroom with a melodramatic sigh.

Peering through the small window in the classroom door, he watched Miss Kelsyan going through the standard machinations. He leaned and looked to the rear of the classroom, taking stock of the typical falderal from the clowning brutes in the back row and the group of girls sitting near Charles Chesterton, the class' two-headed turtle, named after the school's eponym.

Charles was about the only thing that gave Sheldon any enjoyment in class. He liked to imagine that, at night when the school was empty, Mr. Chesterton would extend his secret legs, two yards long or more, and go running about through the dark halls. When he was feeling really frisky, Charles might even slip through a window and head out for a midnight jog around town. That sly, adventurous reptile probably even ran all the way back home sometimes, back to his old stomping grounds at the equator. Although some of the students claimed he was made of wood because he stayed so still during class, Sheldon knew Mr. Chesterton's long-running secret!

Sheldon was swiftly pulled back to reality by a loud burst of laughter coming from inside the classroom, followed by a stern reprimand from Queen Kelsyan. He shook his head, lamenting how schoolboys always sparked so much trouble, throwing erasers and what-not and cracking the most unfunny jokes; while schoolgirls seemed to love nothing more than to pass notes and giggle as if giggling were necessary for their survival. It was all the same nonsense day after day, no real stimulation, no fundamental purpose, and certainly no adventure in any of it whatsoever.

"Ugh." Another sigh of surrender preempted a reluctant, slow turning of the door handle. At the same time however, his feet, seemingly under some spell, like bloodhounds catching a scent, began spinning his torso in the opposite direction, back toward the lizard in the blizzard, toward the alluring light in the doorway. Before he knew it, he was running at top speed for the exit, in pursuit of glorious, forbidden freedom.

Lion Man

"Shel-dunnnn!"

He thought he heard someone call his name as he flung the school doors wide and burst into the open air with explosive ferocity. For all he cared, that name could echo through the halls of Darwin Elementary for all eternity, but he wasn't going to stick around to sign autographs.

The light of the world, contrasted against the dark Darwin halls, blinded the fugitive as he sprung over the steps like a pouncing wildcat, half in flight, trying not to fall on his face—a rocket ship catching fire in the blazing day. Somewhere in the distance an imaginary crowd cheered for him like they did for their hometown hero, Bruce Campbell, during the Tigers-Reds World Series a couple years back when Campbell smashed that terrific home run.

His heart pounded out of his chest as he planted his feet firmly on the sidewalk in a wide stance, arms stretched out as if to welcome the world, eyes closed and face grinning at the sky as if to say, 'Sheldon has arrived!' Like his desert lizard, he took a moment to charge his batteries in the warm sunlight, a long-time prisoner breathing the free air again.

A moment later he was ready to blast off again—down the sidewalk... out of town... all the way to outer space! But as he readied to depart, something anchored him to that spot. Apprehension and indecision snuck up like a serpent, wrapped a firm grip around his ankle, and held him fast. He'd never ditched school before. Now that he'd broken out, he wasn't sure what to do, didn't know which direction to run. Perhaps not in so many words he thought, *Where would a twelve-year-old go to play hooky from school in a bustling borough of the Windy City?* He marinated a beat, shook his head against the urge to run home—"Don't be a chicken!" he growled, mustering his courage.

There must've been a million places to go... if he had the gumption. But where to start? The movie theater? The ice cream shop? The toy store?

"My billfold!" he patted his pockets.

His wallet had been tucked safely in his book bag back in the classroom, and there was certainly no going back for that prisoner-of-war now. Not that it made any difference. *Probably empty, as usual,* he admitted. These days no one had an extra dime, let alone a dollar. He carried the leather pouch as more of an heirloom. It'd been given to him by his grandmother on behalf of his late grandfather, Sigmund, who had worked in a tannery and made the leather wallet with his own leathered hands. After Sigmund's passing, Rae, Sheldon's grandmother, handed down the wallet along with some advice: "One should always keep in one's billfold, at minimum, a one-dollar bill for good luck and prosperity." "Money attracts money, my boy," the grandfolks would say.

Sheldon's father had a different philosophy about allowing children to keep money: Don't. Sheldon's dad, Patterson, did not hold much faith in the capabilities of children, especially his own. Like the kids at Darwin, Sheldon's father deemed his son little more than a silly-hearted dreamer.

Patterson's folks had immigrated from Eastern Europe, with Patterson the first to be born in America. He'd fought in World War I and as a result, carried a hardened heart with very little patience for anyone who expressed discontent over a steady job that provided pay in one's pocket, a hot meal on one's plate, and a sound roof over one's head. Sheldon, unfortunately, was just such a person. He wanted more out of life than a steady job and a hot meal, and for that he was ostracized by his father. But not his mother. Sheldon's mom, Alanna, was supportive of her son's creativity and his big, beautiful dreams. She would tell Sheldon that he could accomplish whatever he set his mind to. Unfortunately, this division set Sheldon's parents at odds, and their constant arguing drove Sheldon ever deeper into his imaginary world of cartoon drawings and daydreams.

○ ○ ○ ○ ○ ○ ○

Out on the sidewalk in front of the school, Sheldon reached into all four pockets one by one, searching for a nickel, even a penny, but finding nothing but lint and holes. Money always seemed to burn right through his pockets. There was always some piece of candy or bubble gum with baseball cards, a comic book, or adventure novel that would catch his eye. In that respect, and that alone, Sheldon was just like every other boy his age.

As he stood at the base of the steps, balancing the weight of his own willing incarceration on one scale and a life daring him to live on the other, it occurred to him that it didn't matter in which direction he ran, so long as he ran—now! Either that or go back inside, and that was most certainly not an option.

Run Shelby! Quick! Before they catch you!

He blasted off. The further he got from school, the more he became suited to the notion that he did not need a destination, he just needed to keep running. He paused a moment in Logan Square Park to marvel at the Centennial Monument before continuing toward one of his favorite haunts.

As he rounded the alley heading to his beloved Logan Theater, running as fast as his appetite for freedom would carry him, he plowed into two street cops casually searching a potential perpetrator for purloined paraphernalia.

Exhausted from running and surprised by the police, Sheldon gasped for air and immediately choked on the thick irony hanging over him like fog. His would-be (could-be, should-be) free life seemed bent on oppression, as if his very spirit had become institutionalized to well-defined boundaries, controls, discipline...

What was I thinking? I just left school? I never do that! I shouldn't have left. I knew it!

One of the policemen reacted swiftly, grabbing the wayward boy by the collar. "Oh, hello there! May I ask why we're running today?"

Sheldon, terribly out of breath, was taken aback by the policeman's politeness. "Now just calm yourself, son. It's okay. Why don't you tell me where you're headed in such a rush."

Sheldon's instinct was to make up a story, some wild excuse, but all he could think of was claiming that a thief had stolen his knees and he kneeded to get them back. This of course made no sense.

"Please, son, where might your parents be? And why are you not in school at this hour, may I ask?"

Sheldon's mind was flipping through his encyclopedia of excuses but nothing stayed long enough to grasp. He wished desperately to hitch a ride with his runaway thoughts to anywhere but there.

"I'm terribly sorry to have to do this son, but if you're not going to answer my questions, you'll have to accompany me to the police station, with all due respect."

Confused by the policeman's manners—*Is this cop trying to be funny?*—Sheldon grew even more tongue-tied. Like a deflating balloon, he surrendered to his capture. Meanwhile, his adrenaline still flowed like fire, burning him up on the inside. The more his mind whirled and twisted, trying to sort out what to do, the more he could feel himself diminishing, turning to naught but ash.

The cop's voice faded along with all the other street noise to an overwhelming buzz. Sheldon dropped his head uncontrollably, as if an invisible spirit had placed a lead crown of shame upon his head. His eyesight blurred to a tunnel of black and white static as he stared fixedly at his ratted shoes, the only thing remaining in his field of vision.

Why did you fly me away like that? he berated the sneakers.

As he stared at his feet, the concrete beneath him liquified to quicksand and he could feel his body sink under the weight of self-pity. Guilt hung from him like sandbags on a dirigible, pulling him ever farther into the mortal mire. This was it, his nightmare coming true! Would he next be dragged off to become dinner for some sinister cannibal of the concrete jungle? It wasn't long before he found himself sunk up to his ears, the sounds of the world now a distant hum, his head vibrating, his body numb. He closed his eyes, tilted his head back to face the sky, and stretched his neck as far as he could to catch one... last... breath. Just before going under, he heard a faint voice.

"Open your eyes, you fuddle-dupper! Don't be so dramatic."

Obeying the pragmatic advice, he reluctantly pried one eyelid open just a slit, just enough to catch a flash from that playful beam of light. It was his luminous guide calling to him again. His eyes shot open in excitement then squinted from the intense brightness. He was alive! Not sinking in quicksand, not fading away...

But still captured. This time the light was coming from some distant alley, perhaps reflecting off a building. Who knew? Just as before, back in the school hallway, his feet became animated under their own ascendancy. His body spasmed and he spun in a wobbly circle before starting in the direction of the mysterious glare. He didn't get far, however. The polite cop was still holding tight to his jacket collar, and he was jerked backward as if hooked to a rubber band.

"Excuse me, son, would you mind holding still, please?"

Sheldon instinctively shook his torso, invoking the old, 'severed-lizard's-tail' trick. It was just enough. The cop tightened his grip on the boy's jacket but the contents slipped away like ice cream left out on the porch in July. As the little devil sped off, the second policeman took chase. Obviously this kid must have stolen something or vandalized something, and this cop was going to nab someone before the day was out, so help him—even if it was just a young boy.

Darting through sidewalk traffic, Sheldon was half crying and half laughing. This was certainly the most trouble he'd ever incited, and though terrified of what consequences awaited him upon capture, the excitement was too alluring. Still confounded as to a destination, especially now with the police bearing down, Sheldon ran in all directions at once, jogging left, darting right, running in circles then doubling back in the opposite direction. He ran out into busy streets, dodging cars and fast-moving trollies—passengers pointing and hollering at the policeman in pursuit of the boy. He ran past street vendors and accidentally bumped into a delivery man who fumbled and dropped his crates of milk, spilling the white gold over the sidewalk, much to the delight of a pack of stray dogs. For a moment, Sheldon felt a jolt of remorse about his recklessness, but a second later his remorse was chomped on, chewed up, and spit out by the beast called Mischievous Thrill.

As he leaped over a pile of boxes—possibly a house for some unfortunate guttersnipe—he looked back to see if the policeman had successfully surmounted the hobo hotel and ran smack into a large, broad man, bringing the shenanigans to immediate arrest. The human wall grabbed hold of the boy firmly, his herculean hands wrapping almost twice around the kid's biceps. Frightened, Sheldon looked up to see a tanned, bucolic face framing sympathetic eyes, asking, 'Why are you running?'

The man wore a thick head of blonde hair that flowed like a river into an unkempt, golden beard. Together, the tangled mop gave the impression of a lion's mane. But this lion bore no long, sharp teeth, Sheldon noted as the man's welcoming smile reassured that all was well. This cat was wearing an army uniform, looking as though he were either off to the war overseas or had just returned. He released Sheldon's left arm but held firmly, yet gently, onto his right. "Slow down there, fella. Where's the fire?"

Sheldon opened his mouth, but as before, failed to push any words out.

"You okay?" the man prodded, tilting his head. Sheldon just stared silently with his mouth agape, so the soldier slowed his speech. "Where... are... your... folks?" Still breathing hard, Sheldon shifted his eyes away from the soldier, back in the direction he'd been running. Noting the boy's preoccupation, the soldier glanced backward, down the sidewalk. "Someone chasin' ya?"

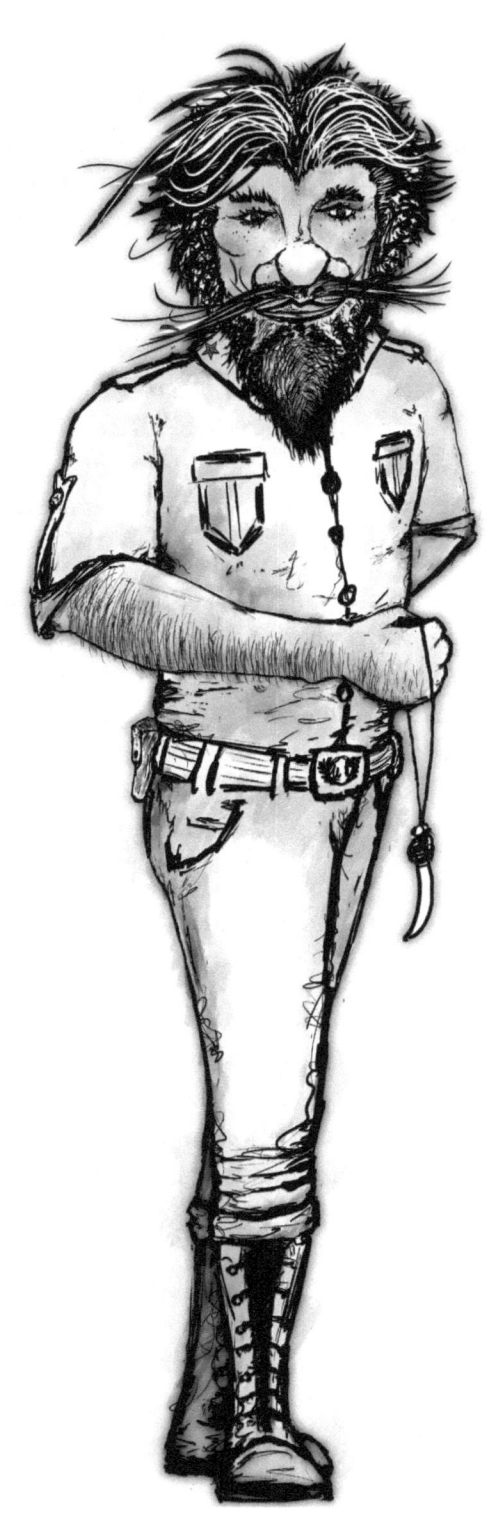

Just then, the tenacious policeman rounded the far corner of the block, out of both breath and patience. Upon seeing the soldier with the apprehended youth, the cop began shoving his way through the crowd, pointing, blowing his whistle, and crying out, "Stop that boy!"

Put off by the gruff manner of the policeman, the soldier turned his attention back to his captive. As he did, he noted the unusual tooth pendant hanging around Sheldon's neck. With his free hand, the man reached down and gently took the pendant in his massive palm for closer inspection.

"Now this is a curious trinket." The man looked Sheldon in the eyes and was met with desperation mixed with a hint of what the lion recognized from years of combat as innocent fear. Taking pity on the boy, the soldier suspended judgment and allowed himself a moment of nostalgia for his own rascally childhood. Then, without realizing, caught in distant recapitulation, the lion-man loosened his grip on the boy's arm. Immediately, Sheldon shook off the giant hand and darted away, but not before turning back with a smile and a wave of gratitude.

That was Sheldon's first encounter with a soldier, and not one he would soon forget—especially since he miscalculated his escape and sped away with his pendant sitting squarely in the palm of the lion-man's hand

"Wait! Hey, kid!" the soldier called out, surprised by the boy's sudden departure, but it was too late. Sheldon wasn't about to stop running so the police could catch him. Unfortunately, the pendant had become entangled in the soldier's fingers as Sheldon wriggled free, and he was too full of adrenaline to feel the chain snap from around his neck as he jerked away.

As the policeman bolted by, he scowled at the soldier for letting the fugitive go. In response, the lion raised his pendant-adorned fist toward Sheldon and cheered, "Give 'em hell, kid!"

A Long Walk

The young outlaw ran until his lungs burned

and his legs felt like noodles, eventually coming to rest in front of a department store with floor-to-ceiling glass walls and fancy gold lettering that shimmered in the late-morning light—a fishing lure attracting schools of sardine-like shoppers...

The stream of patrons swimming in and out of the entryway busied themselves with grown-up tasks, ignoring the goings-on of the natural world persisting around them despite the sterile concrete and steel. Wonderfully crisp, spring air sang sweetly into deaf ears. Brilliant sunlight danced playfully in front of blind eyes.

Insects and birds and rodents scuttled about in anonymity, building bridges connecting islands of life, miniature worlds refusing to submit: a tuft of weeds pushing through eventual cracks in a sidewalk too old and tired to resist; a makeshift life-raft-of-a-bird's-nest sheltering in the crook of a rusted lamp post... Catching his breath, Sheldon paused to admire the miracle of this otherwise invisible world. The more he looked and listened, the more he saw and heard. Even there in the city drab—man's monumental effort to keep the wild spaces out—nature could yet be found for those with eyes to *see* and ears to *listen*.

There he stood on the busy sidewalk, weighing the freedom of the streets against the potential for losing his pursuers amongst the chaos of commerce. From somewhere in his gut, he felt a sudden urge to move on lest he be crushed by a piano, iron safe, or air conditioner falling from an overhead window. Squinting skyward, his hand on his brow in a military salute, he surveyed the windows upon windows stacked like a vertical glass highway stretching to heaven. There were no flying pianos... unless they were invisible flying pianos—those being the most dangerous sort, of course. Still, he felt it best to move along. He calmed his nerves with a deep breath, calmed his disheveled hair with a pass of his hand over his head, then slipped—a lost minnow joining the sardines—into the busy store.

He wandered around for a good amount of time, marveling at all the bright and clean and novel items available to those who could afford such things, which was not his family. Gold and silver necklaces sparkled viciously, 'Keep dreaming, kid,' they scoffed as they came to rest on necks wreathed in the pelts of dead animals. Sheldon shook his head not in envy but in pity, and walked on.

He passed displays of modern conveniences for kitchens and bathrooms, displays of more shoes than feet in the world to fill them, more

hats than heads to hold them, displays advertising luggage and gelato...
That's an odd combination, he scrutinized.

Wandering into a music shop with a plethora of pianos on the
showroom floor, he lightly tapped an ominous tune on the black keys, until
some official-looking lad—a plumber apparently—shooed him away with
a dripping-wet plunger.

He stopped in front of a window to marvel at an array of television
sets, each playing the same show about three bumbling men with silly-
looking haircuts, poking fun at one another and poking each other's eyes,
or trying to, while getting into all sorts of mischief. He lost track of time,
forgetting who and where he was, mesmerized by the glowing light box,
until he noticed the reflection in the television screens. People behind him
were beginning to stare, no doubt curious about a lone child in the city
during school hours. He lowered his head and quickly rejoined the mass of
traffic. Realizing he would no doubt catch the attention of a security guard
eventually, he diverged from the school of nosey fish and slipped through
the nearest exit—which did not spit him out onto the same street from
which he entered.

Here the buildings seemed foreign, much taller than any of the ones
in his Palmer Square neighborhood. They looked like giants, darkening the
streets as they scraped the underbelly of the cosmos, blocking the sun
climbing ever higher on its slow, invisible escalator. The boy's emotions
volleyed between apprehension and amazement at the looming titans,
replacing his thoughts about pursuing policemen with a daydream:

He was the adventurous Jack Spriggins, coursing through the
clouds amongst man-eating giants, golden-egg-laying hens, and magical
singing harps. Occasionally, rays of magnificent sunlight sneaking past the
sleeping giants would shine on him in a spotlight of fortune, endowing him
with a fleeting sense of importance, dare he say *royalty*. But it was not to
last. One particular golden glow became so bright it jolted him out of his
dream like an electric shock.

He immediately recognized the familiar flash as his aberrant
luminous guide. She'd returned, and so he resumed his pursuit of her. He

had to. What choice did he have but to seek out her source, her purpose in contacting him, the reason she kept calling to him? Beyond this he hadn't any plan. He was simply responding to the whispers of the world, the will of nature, the whims of this strange and wonderful guiding glow.

The lack of a plan in his meanderings didn't bother him so much. In fact, he rather enjoyed 'living by the seat of his pants,' going as the wind blew—or in this case, as the sun shined. Normal life for Sheldon wasn't like this. Most days he felt powerless, like the world moved on around him, despite him, regardless, well beyond his control. Such was the catalyst for his incessant daydreaming, because at least with daydreaming one can control what happens... mostly.

This adventure felt different, however. He still felt small and powerless, especially below such impressive buildings, amidst all this street traffic, all these busy people coming and going, with important places to be and things to do. But, small and powerless or not, there he was, entirely by his own free will. He had created his current situation and that was a sort of power, he figured. This time, even if it was by accident, he was pursuing a largely aimless pursuit, following these strange flashes from some invisible heavenly lighthouse spinning in long, slow circles over the earth. In this way, the adventure itself had become its own destination. All he knew was that each time he saw the flash he felt compelled to move, as if she were an old friend prodding him, "Time to go, Sheldon." So, without a real destination but with plenty of energy, he ran on, fueled by the confluence of instinct, light, and this sturdy sidewalk under his feet.

o o o o o o o

He ran until the giants of glass and steel yielded to shorter and longer stone buildings with smaller windows or no windows at all. In places where windows might have been there were large signs or murals painted over brick, identifying manufacturing and processing plants, textile factories, mills, canneries, tanneries, utility stations... The industrial sector, though it felt more familiar, also felt more deserted, less inviting.

Sheldon's run settled to a rhythmic walk as he scrutinized one building after another, becoming ever more familiar with his city so obviously full of fascinating history. How ingenious were the original architects of industry? How skilled were the masons of civilization's foundations? What spirits still haunted these age-old buildings, these serpentine streets? He shivered. The chill of this dark part of town was palpable. He began to miss his jacket, *Which the cops now have*! He frowned, rubbing his arms and hugging himself. Where had his warm, luminous friend gone? His head swiveled like a weathervane in a storm, looking for the spotlight, and for signs that people might be following him. Surely curious eyes must be watching him from within the old warehouses. As usual, no one seemed the least bit interested.

Alone and anonymous he walked on, quietly observing the slow transition of Chicago's industrial sector into quaint, suburban neighborhoods as this strange and wonderful day stretched out, reaching ever farther for new hours to devour.

o o o o o o o

The sun was well past its zenith when Sheldon paused to rehydrate at a park hand-pump fountain. The large city buildings had become a thing of the past, replaced by small mom-and-pop shops, modest houses, and well-groomed green spaces. A group of kids were enjoying a game of basketball. Sheldon wondered if perhaps they too were playing hooky, a thought which made him feel less alone—only slightly, however, for unlike his kind, these kids were suburbanites. There were many things separating him from his peers at Darwin, but in this one thing they were aligned: they loathed the kids from the suburbs. The suburban kids, in due turn, loathed the inner-city kids right back—a mutually agreeable rivalry. He had to admit, however, that he was rather enjoying his walk through suburbia. It was quite nice actually, calm and bright and inviting, like coming home and falling on the couch after a long day. But this place was even more comfortable than the davenport in his living room, for out here there wasn't the constant harangue of the apartment. Here, there were no parents arguing or yelling at one another, or at him. Here his dad wasn't berating and belittling him. Out here, he could breathe.

The fresh perspective yielded a new appreciation for the outer bands of the atom in which he existed. Somewhere a slight *creak* could be heard as his mind expanded. His judgment against suburban Chicagoans, which had felt as normal as putting on the same pair of shoes every day, now felt rather uncomfortable; antiquated now that he thought about it; dare he say constraining for such a mature soul as he.

He stretched his torso to match his broadening mind and stood up tall, looking around. Over his shoulder, he glimpsed something that made his eyes go wide, complimenting a silly grin instantly sweeping across his face as if by brushstroke. An old-fashioned soda fountain shop was calling his name. He stopped in his tracks and drooled at the thought of a sundae or root beer float, until his eyes yanked his attention away from the sugary treats to something even sweeter: motorcycles!

Keeping good company with the soda parlor was a repair garage where several shiny, newer-looking bikes sat on display. The young fugitive began toying with the notion of jumping on one of them and speeding off into the sunset. There was only one problem with his plan... Actually, there were at least a dozen problems with this plan, one being that the sun wouldn't be setting for another five or six hours.

"Okay, so maybe putter off into the *eventual* sunset," he chuckled.

The bigger problem was that Sheldon didn't know *how* to drive a motorcycle. *But I could learn! Yes! I could get a job in the repair shop right here and now! Never go back to school!* He figured he could become a master mechanic and restore old Indians, Husqvarnas, and Harley-Davidsons to their full glory. He could build himself a safari-ready enduro and ride across the African continent on the ultimate two-wheeled adventure. *Yes! That's it!* he mused. He would seek out the great Zulu king and teach him to ride a wheelie. He would race a cheetah for top land speed record. He would ride to the top of Mount Kilimanjaro and proclaim from the roof of Africa for all to see and hear, that the great Sheldon Silvers was the first motorcyclist in history to triumph over the wild continent!

"Well, that settles it," he wagged a finger at destiny. "The bike will have to be a Triumph!" And when his great escapade was utterly spent, having conquered the most incredible features and elements—zebras and elephants—the world's most exotic continent could throw at him, he would sell his trophy bike and buy himself an airplane, fly off over the savannah, across the Rift Valley and the dark Congo, out over the vast Atlantic, to his next grand adventure in the uncharted Amazon! Or perchance he might go east to the Himalayas! Just one problem (just one?): he didn't know how to fly a plane.

Onward, Sheldon noticed other boys about his age hard at work baling hay or delivering newspapers on bicycles or scrubbing car tires at fueling stations. He felt slightly jealous and wondered why he couldn't drop out of school and take up the occupation of drawing and writing stories. His father wouldn't object to him dropping out so long as he went to work at the bakery full-time... *Yeah, never mind. I think I'll stay in school, thanks.* As he strolled, he entertained himself, humming a tune to narrate his journey.

Wandering by a pungent delicatessen,
Cuts of pork and poultry on display,
I shake my head and lament with sorrow,
How innocent animals are treated in this way.
I pass a barbershop and watch with glee,
As a man with double nose and triple chin,
Sips a glass of golden grown-up tea,
While taking in a shave and mustache trim.
A general store painfully reminds me,
I've had no lunch and now am starving hungry.
Oh, how I wish I had a nickel or a penny,
To buy myself a chocolate or some candy.

A shoe sales and cobbler shop followed the general store and Sheldon, soles feeling worn thin from so much walking, smirked at the thought of popping in to get his feet repaired. A large mercantile hobby shop rounded out commercial row, queuing several dozen homes scattered here and there, each with nice big yards, most with laundry hung out to dry, some with small play sets for children.

The quaint town shops and cookie-cutter houses became less frequent until, eventually, the surroundings opened to vast stretches of farmland with the occasional ranch house stuck in the far corner of a windrow-lined plot. The serenity of the countryside soothed any remaining anxiety Sheldon felt as a result of running away from school and the subsequent police chase. Though he had never lived anywhere but the city, he felt right at home there in farm country. He even found himself chatting with the odd cow or flock of sheep. Upon seeing some horses running and playing in a nearby field, he traded in his African motorcycle fantasy for an Arabian horseback fantasy.

Long robes of silk flowing wildly in his wake as he races along sandy peaks in an endless sea of scorching dunes. A merciless sun works overtime, extracting every last bead of moisture from both rider and stallion. They're a raging haboob, moving as one, like a cobra on the hunt, driven by mad thirst, carving a disappearing trail atop drifting sand in relentless pursuit of the bazaar at the oasis. Giant palm trees sway in the distance, calling to them like sirens at sea signaling safe harbor. And yet, the distant sanctuary, shimmering in the sweltering heat, tenaciously holds fast to an ever-elusive horizon. Could it be... a mirage???

"Nooooo!" Sheldon bellowed in a dramatic whisper, arms flapping in the air. He broke into a laugh, quite satisfied with his *Arabian Nights* detour, and walked on. After some time, the endless farmland became rather monotonous and his gaze drifted lazily south, fixating on his shuffling shoes.

'Swoosh, swoosh, swoosh,' went his sneakers, back and forth, back and forth. His mind became lost in the rhythmic pendulum of his feet swinging in step with the cracks in this persistent pavement, this walkway of wonders that had carried him from the city, through suburbia, beyond rural Chicago, and out past the Illinois farm fields.

"Careful now," he mused. "Mustn't step on the crack or we'll break mamma's... Oops! Sorry ma!" he laughed, enjoying this late afternoon stroll, a nowhere man all alone in nowhere land.

'Swish, swish,' sounded his pants as they shuffled.

'Swoosh, swoosh,' replied his sneakers in a textile discourse about the simple meaning of...

Life? What's this? He stopped and bent down, picking up what appeared to be a wooden jigsaw puzzle piece lying lonely on the sidewalk. As he did, he suddenly became aware of the missing pendant no longer hanging around his neck, which otherwise might have brushed across his face when he bent over.

"Wha?! NO!" He stood bolt upright, grasping his shirt collar, patting himself all over, desperately searching in case the pendant had become entangled in his clothes somewhere. *It must've fallen off when I was running*, he told himself, lamenting the loss of his unique treasure. He turned and for half a second considered going back for it but quickly conceded there would be no point. It was gone.

Feeling sad and angry, he bent down and picked up the lonely puzzle piece—a mediocre consolation— along with some stones. He took to chucking rocks at an old tin can by the side of the road and that made him feel a little better.

Examining the puzzle piece, half covered in dirt that didn't want to come off no matter how much he spat on it, he could see that it was faded blue with some red speckled here and there. The word 'image' was stamped on it in cracked white lettering with the 'e' at the end smudged such that it looked more like an 'i'.

"Image. Well, duh," he scoffed, turning the piece over. The back side was blank, covered in more dirt than the front. It was impossible to tell into what larger picture this piece might fit. There were so many possibilities. Sheldon instantly empathized with this lonely fragment, seemingly minuscule and insignificant and already labeled in the most obvious way. Yet, certainly there was more to the story. Certainly this individual piece contributed in a unique way to a bigger picture. Certainly without this particular piece the whole story would forever be incomplete.

"Interesting." He placed the piece in his pocket and stood up, looked out over the fields and considered the bigger picture into which he fit. He faced the low sun in the west, whose diminished light now gave the wheat fields a warm, golden glow, and he thought about his life in that moment. This boy, this unique puzzle piece, despite still not having a defined purpose for leaving school and walking so far away, was overcome with the sense that things were slowly coming together, not falling apart.

That was the moment he became aware of the missing road. The tarmac had apparently quit some time back, and this concrete walkway on which he stood was now chaperoned only by rough gravel. He contemplated the absence of asphalt and the absence of traffic, the absence of houses and towns and people.

Wrapped in an eerie sense of aloneness, his gaze drifted upwards. The sun had only another hour or so before it would head off to shine on some other, distant land. The thought of impending darkness startled him and he began running again—slowly at first, hesitation providing resistance as though he were moving through water. Overcoming doubt with a renewed sense of adventure, he was soon running as fast as he could, trying to race the sunlight, to keep the night at bay. Eventually, he conceded that he was only racing further into darkness and slowed to a jog before stopping altogether.

Struggling to catch his runaway breath, he glanced back in the direction he'd come. Instantly a fog of sadness fell over him, the weight of which sent him to his knees. There he knelt, wondering about his predicament. No doubt there would come a time when he would miss the attention of his troubled family, the comfort and safety of his noisy home, the warm yet small meals, even the militarized routine of Darwin. But not yet. As unappealing as the thought of returning home was, even more compelling was the feeling that he would be giving up on something were he to turn back. What exactly, he did not know, but he could feel it, deep in his gut. He had to keep going despite the darkness creeping toward him from the far end of the sidewalk like ruffians on a playground stalking their prey. He could feel his courage draining. That's when he saw it again: his luminous friend flashing a timely ray of hope. It was so obviously the same beam of light that had awakened him to this fateful day, had called him out and away from school, had guided him safely away from the police, compelled him all this way out into the world so very far from home.

"What are you?" he whispered.

The light twinkled secretively, excitedly, as if it had a present hiding behind its back and couldn't wait for him to open it.

To the west, emerging from a low-hanging cloud, the setting sun flashed a complimentary glow, signaling its retirement and passing of the torch to the mysterious guiding light. In response, like an eager youth entrusted with an important task, the easterly illumination shined brighter than ever, brandishing a steady glow, no longer intermittent and fleeting, no longer obscured by dropped curtains, closed doors, or giant buildings. Sheldon stood to witness his brilliant friend, and as he did, he caught sight of the bigger picture. His gaze lazily drifted out over the remarkably vast and uncurated landscape, no roads to define it or fences to corral it. This was the first time he could recall being able to see all the way to the natural horizon in every direction. All around him was open land and endless sky as far as the eye could see. He felt his soul take a long, deep breath in a way entirely new. Inside, a voice comforted him with inaudible words, like a friend placing a gentle hand around his shoulder. Reassured, he turned away from the sorrowful walk home and embraced the exciting walk to...

...to wherever this rogue sidewalk would lead.

A Light in the Attic

Sheldon was starving, exhausted, and terribly thirsty. But he also felt renewed by this novel experience of soul freedom, the excitement of untold adventures propelling him toward this mysterious spotlight still shining on him as if he were the main event...

He was too excited to walk, and so he ran (mostly skipped actually, but that's our secret), until the source of the light came into view, stopping him instantly in his tracks. The gravel road from town had devolved into a narrow, red dirt two-track leading right to the only house he'd seen for what must have been hours.

There it is!

Just up ahead stood a magnificent old farmhouse, painted all white save for a faded red roof, from the top of which protruded a narrow attic, brilliantly lit from the inside, giving it the look of a lighthouse on a cliff. The tall grass surrounding the house bent and swayed in the wind like waves on an ocean. Despite being nowhere near the sea, sounds of gulls and crashing waves could be heard in the distance. Sheldon's imagination was winding up. He spotted a clipper ship coursing the turbulent farmland, bowing to one side then the other in respect to the wind and waves.

Pirates!

Beyond the house he could see the sidewalk stretching onward, disappearing into a dark forest, beckoning him to deeper adventure. He looked back from where he'd come. There appeared to be nothing in either direction, nothing but the farmhouse. Knocking at the front door now while he still had a sliver of light by which to escape if necessary seemed his only option if he didn't want to sleep outside, alone in the cold. Besides, he was eager to finally pin down the source of this perplexing light.

The setting sun cast a warm flush over the house, putting the boy's mind at ease with a hunch that the nicest family lived there. He imagined a father with a gentle smile and kind eyes, washing up for supper after a long and tiring but rewarding day in the fields. The man's dear wife was brushing an egg-white glaze atop an apple pie before setting it in the oven to crisp, their two children already seated quietly at the table. She was the sweetest mom, always attentive and never cross. The kids were obedient and well-mannered. The wayward youth wouldn't be an intrusion at all. He would be welcomed graciously and would be well-looked-after until his parents could come collect him. Surely these good folks would have a telephone he could use. If not, of course Mr. Thompson (Sheldon had already named the family) would drive him home first thing after supper.

Sheldon was convinced. He pushed the white picket gate open and began walking confidently to the front door. The sound of steel clicking behind him made him jump and then freeze at the thought that he'd made a terrible mistake and now stood at the dangerous end of a cocked rifle. He slowly glanced back.

"Just the gate," he reassured himself with a slight grin, admitting that perhaps he'd been too liberal with his imagination as of late. Continuing toward the house, he licked his lips in anticipation of a glorious meal. As he climbed the porch steps—careful not to trip on the old, twisting wood treads, curling upward at the ends, trying to break free—he noticed a peculiar wooden sign hanging on the door.

"'Jays dwell here and sunbeams too...' Hmm, wonder what that means," he queried to the evening. In the distance, a jaybird screeched. He might have been frightened by the ominous reply were it not for his stomach growling, convincing him that he could already smell the apple pie baking in the oven. "My goodness!" he delighted quietly as he gave the Marley knocker a few good raps before stepping back and straightening his posture for presentation to the Thompson family.

No one answered.

They must be busy laughing and sharing stories of the day. His stomach grumbled, complaining about the delay, teased by imaginings of roast chicken with perfectly crisped golden-brown skin the color of the countryside, mounds of creamed potatoes complimented with pats of melting butter slipping down like sleds on snow, tugboat mushrooms floating in meandering rivers of gravy, freshly-felled trees of broccoli waiting to be milled alongside whole logs of red and white carrots...

The carrots he could stomach, but he'd never been fond of broccoli. "Yuck! ...But, given our famished state..." his imagination argued, "...And of course we wouldn't want to be rude..." It was settled, he would even be enjoying his vegetables tonight.

You're daydreaming again.

He shook himself back to reality, realizing he'd probably been standing on the porch for several long minutes, gorging on naught but illusion.

What's taking them? The pie should be out of the oven by now!

He wiped the drool from his lip and hammered the brass knocker, this time much harder. Taking a step back, he held his breath. Behind him, from below the distant tree line, the last slivers of sunlight whispered, "Farewell and good luck," as darkness charged over the eastern hills like a migration of crows.

As the lighting over the landscape changed, so did the boy's perception of the farmhouse. The warm light that made him feel safe had turned stale and cold. Sheldon's brilliant and beautiful lighthouse had suddenly gone lifeless as if turned to stone by the terrible Medusa. Forgetting the food momentarily, he jumped from the porch and peered up at the attic window from where the beacon light had originated, hopeful that the friendly beam would reassure his fading spirit. But the window had also gone dark like the surface of a northern lake in winter—not frozen, but completely still and silvery—mirror-like.

Had it all been an illusion?

He had to concede the illogic of a single light from the attic of a rural farmhouse being seen from miles away, deep in the urban labyrinth, unobstructed by trees or buildings or telephone poles or chimneys...

"Dang it!" He jumped onto the porch and in a fit of frustration and desperation, pounded on the door, nearly breaking through the aged wood planks. Immediately he regretted his outburst as this would certainly upset the otherwise mild-mannered Mr. Thompson.

In a panic he turned and bolted from the house, running as fast as he could back down the walkway. He didn't bother with the gate, choosing instead to launch himself over the fence. But as he pushed off the top of the pickets with both hands, flinging his legs into the air uncontrollably, one of his pantlegs became ensnared in a bush of climbing roses (also trying to escape) and he tumbled to the ground, hitting the back of his head hard on the concrete before coming to rest, face down on the sidewalk.

For several long minutes—or perhaps much longer—he lay motionless from pain, dizziness, and fear, hoping that he was at least below the sightline of Mr. Thompson's rifle irons. Surely the man of the house must now be standing guard with his firearm trained on the commotion in the twilight, ready to defend his beloved family... and his dinner, which was now getting cold thanks to this ridiculous interruption!

Emotion swelled in Sheldon's eyes with the realization that he would never get to enjoy the delicious roast chicken and the company of this sweet family. Succumbing to exhaustion, frustration, and hunger, tears flowed uncontrollably and he slammed his fists on the concrete, feeling thoroughly betrayed by his closest friend: this cruel, overactive imagination.

Where the Sidewalk Ends

As he lay on the sidewalk, too angry and afraid to move, Sheldon felt a soothing warmth seep up through his clothes, calming his nerves. The sunlight that had been absorbed by the concrete throughout that hard but rewarding day was now radiating back out like memory...

Closing his eyes, he calmed his breath and recalled the events of the day: the repellent babble inside his house, the droning nonsense of school, the exciting police chase, the discovery of new places and new freedoms, and now this wide-open space with room for his spirit to roam. But had he roamed too far?

With a sigh, he whisper-sang:

> *Here lies Sheldon.*
> *What a life he almost had!*
> *Born a playful pup,*
> *He was warned never to grow up.*
> *But he grow'd up just the same,*
> *And departed without a name,*
> *And that's all that ever happened to the lad!*

With another sigh and a shift in his posture to align his body with the uneven sidewalk, he carefully placed an arm behind his throbbing head and looked up at the billowing clouds of dusk. The first stars of the evening were clocking in for the night shift, countless shades of blue blending ever darker as this most peculiar day yielded to untold adventures of night.

The sidewalk felt so warm and comforting he thought he might just sleep right there were it not for his restless mind attempting to reel in the bizarre circumstance of the light in the attic. Finding that task nothing short of impossible, Sheldon surrendered his thoughts, deciding instead to admire the appearance of ever more stars in the sky, gathering like a reunion of old friends.

Looking up at the heavens he was reminded of a curious story his mother used to read to him and his kid sister. He imagined himself as the boy prince living on a small star with his only friend, a delicate rose. He recalled images of the prince traveling from planet to planet in search of a cure for his ailing friend, his soulmate, his—

WHAT IN THE COSMOS WAS THAT?!

With a jolt, he sat up and watched as something rocketed by just overhead, flying low and fast across the sky.

"Smokes!" he gasped, tracing the object as it sailed away in the direction where the sidewalk led, to the now-very-dark forest. The thing was soaring too low and looked too small to be an airplane, but it was much too large to be a bird—any bird he knew of anyway. Forgetting the pain in his head he jumped to his feet and took a step towards the trees, then paused, unsure what to do. Thinking he heard a faint cry for help, he sputtered forward, little by little, listening to the distress call trail off in the wake of the puzzling flying thing, over the trees and out of sight.

Unable to resist his lust for adventure, his walk turned to a full sprint until the grip of fear squeezed the courage from him like juice from a lemon. His run slowed to a putter, sneakers dragging on the sidewalk for brakes, before he eventually stopped still. But not from fear as it turned out. Instead, he was halted by a sudden realization that ensnared his curiosity.

He glanced down at his feet. He looked to his left and then to his right. He looked behind him and then spun around in a circle. The farmhouse was no longer within view. There were no buildings or even building lights to be seen anywhere. Even the dirt road was gone. He was surrounded by tall, dry weeds so blonde they appeared to glow in the moonlight. He found himself smack in the middle of an open field, guarded in the distance by primeval forest. Yet, despite nothing but fields and forest and wildland, the sidewalk remained.

There he stood, a small boy on a lonely sidewalk in the middle of nowhere, his only company a handful of stars in a fledgling night sky and the chirping of a solitary bird bathing contently in the crescent moonlight. The setting felt magical and welcoming in a way that helped assuage his fear, and he was suddenly compelled to seek out the ultimate destination of this curiously persistent pathway.

He took a few steps, testing his resolve. Feeling brave, the intrepid explorer trudged on, marveling at his surroundings and imagining what wonders awaited at the concrete terminus.

Surely it must lead to something important, he reasoned with an excitement that catalyzed an increasingly brisk pace. *After all, who would put all this work into such a nice sidewalk for nothing?* He wondered if it might pass all the way through the dark forest. *Perhaps it goes all the way to Lake Michigan or the Mississippi River. I know! I'll bet it goes to—*

SPLISH!

He stopped, his back foot still on solid sidewalk, his front bathing in the shallow end of a boggy marsh.

"UGH!" He tossed his head back and rolled his eyes, gaze eventually settling on a peculiar wooden sign just above him, to his right. On the sign was painted the obvious warning, 'Sidewalk Ends,' in clear, bold lettering. He stood for a moment staring at the pithy guidepost, one foot soaking in a swamp, the other still connected—albeit by many miles— to the city, to home. He slowly withdrew his foot from the puddle, shook off the loose mud and water, and planted his soggy shoe firmly back on what remained of civilization.

Home, he thought, *where mother makes me wash my hands and father makes constant demands; where sister yells and cries, and inspiration withers... and dies.*

He looked at the sign, looked at the forest, looked at his sorry, wet foot, then glanced back in the direction of home. "No. Can't go back. Notchet." *I wanna see what's out there. I want to explore. There must be something in the world for me. There must be something more!*

He looked down again at the puddle.

"Oh, hello."

Staring back at him was an upside-down reflection of his youthful face dancing in the ripples, illuminated by the rising moon.

"Maybe *I* am the reflection and *you* are right-side up? Perhaps in another world, you are *liked* for being weird, or maybe you're not weird at all. Maybe in another world, you're normal and it's weird *not* to be weird, to *not* imagine and daydream and make-believe and..." His words trailed off.

Standing there at the threshold to the wilderness, the edge of the unknown, swamp water draining from his left shoe, he might have been scared out of his wits were it not for a decent moonlight penetrating the canopy, inspiring a calming chirp-song from the persistent midnight bird. A grove of fascinatingly twisted oaks appeared as moonbeam dripped over the landscape like acrylic on a black canvas. The forest now seemed more familiar than frightening, and there was an odd scent of peppermint in the air (which is always reassuring, wouldn't you agree?).

"So, this is where the sidewalk ends," he spoke out loud to the forest. "Now what?"

As if in response, he suddenly heard again the cry for help and was jolted from his peppermint chill. Had he any notion of what was to transpire, he might've paused to reconsider. He might've turned and gone home. But how was he to know?

He stared up at the sign that called out a clear and final transition between the known world and the mysteries beyond, as if to look civilization square in the eye to say goodbye, and then deliberately and confidently stepped off the sidewalk into the unknown...

...being careful not to step in the soggy marsh again.

Falling Up

Once free from the predetermined pathway, Sheldon stood motionless, holding his breath to see if he would implode or maybe get hauled off by some wild beast. But nothing happened. It turned out that the dark, scary woods, like most people he encountered, couldn't have cared less about him. He exhaled at the anticlimax of what he considered to be a symbolic and monumental achievement, and couldn't help but feel disappointed that there wasn't some great, universal celebration at his triumph of shedding the constructs of authority, breaking the bonds of discipline, cutting the cords of—

Wait. What's happening?

He suddenly felt himself shedding something much more tangible than authority: gravity!

As if under some spell, his feet lifted off the ground. He scrambled wildly, grasping for any tree branch within reach, finding naught but air.

"Hey! Whoa! Aaaaah! Wait... WAAAIIIT! HELLLP!" Now *he* was the one calling for help as he realized he was floating up like a helium balloon cut loose at a party. Gravity—or some force like it—was pulling on him but entirely in the wrong direction. At some good distance off the ground he was finally able to grab hold of a small branch, but that only served to slow him down momentarily before the branch gave way, snapping off the tree and smacking him on the head in a bon voyage love tap of, "Good luck out there, kid!"

There was no resisting the force pulling him away from the Earth. Thus, he sped faster and faster outward, onward, upward, falling freely up, up, up at near terminal velocity when suddenly—

CRASH!

He landed hard on something—or rather *in* something, something that was moving, something that was flying, something that smelled of burnt coffee and old socks.

The Festoon Brigade

"What was that?"

"Uhhh... I think we just caught a bird!"

"Well, give it 'a me so's I can add 'er to the stew!"

Sheldon landed in what felt like (and smelled like) a pile of laundry. He tried to stand up but immediately stumbled in response to the zigzagging of the flying object in which he found himself. Tripping over something hard, he fell back into the pile of sundries: shirts, pants, socks... *Is that... underwear?*

With the constant jolting and fumbling about, he became entangled in the linens, unable to see where he was or what was going on. The more he struggled the more the laundry clung to him foxtails. But there were more than just clingy clothes in this pile. Items that felt like books, blocks, pots and pans kept tramping his toes, knocking his knees, and whacking him upside the head. He yelled out in frustration, "AAARGH!"

"Whoa, now! That ain't no bird!" said an anxious voice.

"Well don't just stand there, grab holda it!" said another, more bossy voice.

From within the laundry pile, Sheldon felt a hand grab his ankle and give a tug before quickly letting go.

"Hey!" he protested.

"It's massive! I ain't gettin' near it!"

"Well, what is it?!" asked the bossy voice.

"Here, hit it with this," said another, holding out a large wooden spoon.

Sheldon felt a rapping on his shoulder, a poke in his midsection, and a prod to his legs. "Quit it!" he demanded, grunting and thrashing about, trying to fight off both the laundry and the incessant poking.

"Ahhh! It's a monster!" shrieked one of them.

"Abandon ship!" yelled another.

"The Festoon's been compromised! Every flyer for theyself!" cried a third.

"HELP!" All three called out in unison amongst a great deal of commotion and running about. Three thumps followed by a loud crash rocked the vessel enough to knock Sheldon over again. Upon landing, his eye found a hole in the clothes pile, providing his first glimpse of his surroundings. Reaching out, he grabbed hold of something solid and pulled himself up to get a look at the scene, astonished to discover that he appeared to be flying in some sort of open-topped airplane shaped oddly like a shoe!

A flash of light in the distance ensnared his attention. It was the same farmhouse maybe a hundred feet or so below them, fading into the darkness, and the light in the attic was on! Once again shining brightly, once again a cheerful beacon in an otherwise utterly irksome night.

"What?!" He grabbed his head to keep it from spinning off, then stole a second glance to make sure he wasn't seeing things. Sure enough, the light in the attic was inexplicably glowing once more. And then, as if winking, the light flashed off and back on again in one last goodbye before passing beyond view.

Confusion and disorientation allowed him to forget for a moment that he was flying in a shoe-thing with three unknown creatures, and Sheldon's attention drifted to the dark expanse of the night sky, settling uneasily on the great mass of lights well beyond the farm.

Must be Chicago.

He locked his thoughts on the fading skyline and watched the lights slip beyond view as the vessel sailed ever higher, up through the low clouds of this impossible spring evening. A cloud of loneliness descended over him until a gentle nudge from a curious breeze—more peppermint—reminded him that there were others on board this shoe-ship-thing.

Or were there? Where did they go? He looked around nervously but saw no one.

"They're gone," he whispered cautiously, mind racing. *I frightened them away. They all jumped overboard!* "Ha! Triumph!" he exclaimed to the night, before pausing to scratch his head. "Now what?" His eyes shifted, taking stock of the situation.

(We already established that Sheldon didn't know how to fly a plane. He *certainly* didn't know how to fly a shoe!)

Hang on! What's this?

Three lumps lay on the floor of the ship, all about his size, perhaps a smidge smaller, each with a long beard and different style of hat, and all sleeping, apparently. That, or dead.

They're like Cinderella's dwarves, he thought. *No, that's Sleeping Beauty... Whatever.*

He glanced about the ship, wondering how in the world the thing was flying, especially given that the crew appeared to be unconscious on the floor.

"Hey!" he yelled at the three dwarf-looking lumps. His hands jerked to his mouth to keep any more nonsense from spilling out, realizing there could be more of them hiding and that he should probably exercise a tad more stealth.

Doncha think you oughta maybe tie 'em up first and THEN wake 'em? he argued to himself.

"Well, where might I find some rope?" he replied aloud.

How about a shoelace? himself answered.

He looked around and noticed a thick rope weaving in and out of small portholes at the ship's sides like laces in a shoe, one end dangling conveniently at Sheldon's feet. He grabbed the rope and dragged it to where the sleeping lumps lay. But as he did, the rope became taut and— *WHOOSH!*—the entire ship pitched steeply to one side. The unexpected shift threw Sheldon off balance and he stumbled across the deck, arms waving, searching for something to hold onto. All he could find was the rope already in his hands, so he tugged on that for support. Unfortunately, the rope turned out to be a control line for the ship, and the more he pulled, the more the ship pitched to one side. The pitching caused him to stumble further and pull harder on the rope, and so on in a self-reinforcing catastrophe.

As the ship listed further and further, threatening to tip completely over, everything onboard tumbled chaotically across the ship's deck, including the three bearded lumps, who rolled around like logs on a river barge. Their charade—opossums feigning lifelessness to avoid being eaten by the fox—was now very much over. One by one they sounded expressions of alarm as they tried not to fall out of their ship.

Sheldon, being much less accustomed to flying, or sailing, or whatever this was, lost his footing and careened overboard. By sheer dumb luck the shoelace rope became wrapped around his leg, so instead of falling to his doom, he simply dangled below the ship like an anchor—though he was screaming much louder than an anchor. The one advantage Sheldon had, hanging in mid-air like that, was he no longer had to worry about trying to stay on board, for the flying thing was nearly upside down and the other crew members were having a heck of a time staying in.

"Hang on!" one of them cried.

"Stay in!" another added.

"I'm going to be sick!" the third yelled.

From his vantage point, suspended in mid-air, Sheldon marveled as one of the crew members popped up and began deftly maneuvering about the inverted ship like a spider in a web. The small figure swiftly retrieved the port-side control rope and began heaving and wrenching on it methodically. His efforts countered the erratic tugging on the starboard line by a dangling Sheldon, bobbing around like a yo-yo in space. Almost instantaneously, the ship began to right itself. As it spun back to right-side-up, the rope tied to Sheldon's leg became taut, flinging him back on board with a whip-like crash. The little man quickly grabbed Sheldon's rope and, together with the rope already in his grasp, yanked both lines as if bringing a runaway horse to a halt, smoothing the turbulence and correcting the ship's attitude. The attitude of her crew, however, was not so easily corrected.

As everyone got settled, dusting off the chaos and taking stock of their limbs, one of the long beards spoke up. "Right then! Who's hungry? Mulligan stew anyone?"

"Aaarrrgh!" the other one yelled, lunging at the boy intruder. Sheldon looked up to see the small person who had just saved them, flying through the air at him.

"Humpf!" Sheldon gasped as the stout brute landed on top of him with the weight of several wet sandbags. Instantly, a riotous rasslin' match ensued.

Despite Sheldon's young age, he was pretty scrappy, having had plenty of practice defending himself on the schoolyard. The little squab attacking him was also a skilled tumbler but was on the small side. Although clearly having the weight advantage, the attacker must've been at least a full head shorter than Sheldon.

"Wallop 'im!" cried one of the onlookers.

"Gragurflumpum!" shouted another with a mouth full of stew.

"Wait, who you rootin' fer?" said the first.

"The big one!" said the second, swallowing the soup in one gulp.

"Yeah, me too! ...Wait, which one's the big one?"

There was a pause in heckling as the two cheerleaders pondered for whom they should be cheering. Meanwhile, as the wrestlers continued their epic battle, they became entangled once more in the mess of sundries strewn about the vessel, including Sheldon's nemesis: the dubious laundry pile!

"Well, I s'pose we ought to root fer the one that wins. That would make the most sense, I think," said the soup-eater, taking his now empty bowl and placing it atop his head like a helmet.

"Right. Uh, which one's that?" said the other.

The two rasslers were having a tough time unrav'lin' themselves from one another, and from the clingy clothes. Eventually one of them stood up, tossed a nightshirt off his head, and pointed a large wooden spoon like a sword at the lump still lying on the floor, buried under the laundry.

With his mighty spoon in hand, after taking a moment to catch his breath, the stout man bellowed, "As captain of this here shoe, and commander of the Flying Festoon Brigade, I insist that you, oh mighty trespasser, show yerself and state yer purpose at once, or face the consequences!"

Frustrated and humiliated, Sheldon weighed the option of having another go at the furry, wee captain, muttering under his breath from under the laundry pile, "Captain, my eye! Shoe captain, is it?"

"Yeah, that's right!" replied the man, straightening himself as tall as he could and jabbing the spoon at the air triumphantly.

"Who flies a shoe? That's absurd!" Sheldon angrily discharged the clothes and jumped up, revealing his full size. "My name's Sheldon Silvers and I am NOT a trespasser!" The onlookers reeled and gasped. They'd seen the trespasser only in fleeting glimpses, bouncing around the ship and wrestling with the captain. This was their first good look at the intruder. They half expected to see a grotesque monster with claws and fangs and spikes on its back. (Like Sheldon, they too had overactive imaginations.) Instead, there stood a rather plain-looking kid.

"My word!" exclaimed the soup-muncher, now stirring a large pot with agitated vigor and wearing an expression of amazement. "Uh, would you like some soup, young man?"

"Zip it, Pots!" retorted the captain, whipping the wooden spoon around and pointing it menacingly at his compadre standing over the cauldron, who immediately ducked behind the steaming pot. The captain then swung the spoon back to the boy. "What do you want with my ship?" he demanded.

Sheldon cocked his head sideways and squinted. After a momentary staring contest, he shifted his defiant stare to the person standing to the captain's left, taking stock of the three adversaries (four if you count the laundry).

"Careful, Tick, he's eyeballin' ya!" said the stew chef, still crouching behind the rampart cauldron. At that nonsense, Sheldon shot a razor-sharp glare at the chef, and they locked eyes for a moment before the cook retreated further behind his pot, not wanting to incur the wrath of this unpredictable wayward drifter, this wild-eyed celestial gypsy.

"Ha! Pots, yuh look like when ya accident'ly woke that sleeping dragon, throwing stones into his cave. Where was that again? Oh yeah! Mount Berfelda—"

"Enough, Tick!" scolded the captain.

Sheldon noted the captain's gruff manner, along with the fear in the soup chef's eyes. Wanting to put an end to all the puffed-up posturing, he decided to soften his defenses and extend an olive branch. "You know, I think I *would* like some of your soup, Mr. Soup Man." He then shot the captain a look of, 'Take that, you bully!'

Chef Picklepots transformed his look of terror into an ear-to-ear grin as he stood tall with pride and delighted, "Ha, d'ja hear that, Tick? He called me 'Mr. Soup Man'!"

"Yeah. Almost sounds like Superman!" Together, the crew member called Tick—short for Tickletoes—and the soup chef, Pick—short for Picklepots—broke out in laughter, a common occurrence with those two.

"Enough! Both of you!" interjected the bossy captain. The two chucklers instantly snapped quiet, but that didn't last long. Their unsinkable, jovial nature being what it was, they couldn't help but regrow silent smiles after their grumpy captain looked away, turning his attention back to the intruder. "I'm captain of this crew, and there'll be no soup... or anything else... until we get to the bottom of this... this stowaway-ness!"

Picklepots whispered, "I'd rather get to the bottom of this stewpot-ness." Tickletoes giggled. Captain Fickleface missed the remark.

Sheldon, who also didn't catch the tension-cutting comment, wasted no time defending himself. "I told you already, I am not a trespasser! And I am not a stowaway! I don't want your ship. I don't want anything to *do* with your ship. I'm here by accident. I simply fell into it as I was—"

The captain hoisted a skeptical eyebrow like a pirate's Jolly Roger, a clear warning. Pointing the wooden spoon at the boy, who had trailed off, the captain pressed slowly, "As you were *what?*"

"As I was... um... falling?" Sheldon shrugged.

"You were falling? From where? Ain't no treetops or mountains up that high 'round them's parts... buildings neither. Did you happen to drop out of a hot air balloon then?"

"No." Sheldon hesitated a moment before proceeding. "I was falling... um... up." The boy smiled sheepishly at the captain.

"Falling... up?"

"Yup. That's right."

"You're a tootin' liar!" the captain wagged his spoon wildly in front of the boy's face, trying to look as threatening as possible, his small stature and ridiculous weapon not helping his cause.

Sheldon threw up his hands to protect himself from the wagging spoon and inadvertently swatted the thing right out of the captain's hand, sending it zipping across the ship with destructive velocity, striking the soup man square in the mouth, knocking the smile right off of *his* face and sending it over to his friend Tick's face, who thought the whole incident was hilarious.

"OWWW! My TOOF!" Picklepots wailed as he covered his mouth with one hand and held out the other, palm up, displaying a large tooth, tears streaming down his chubby cheeks.

"Oops!" Sheldon covered his mouth sympathetically.

Immediately, the captain ran over to console his friend. As he comforted the soup chef, he glared at the assailant with hate-filled eyes. The incident had confirmed his suspicions that this nefarious mister Sheldon character was out for blood.

"Tickletoes!" yelled the captain. "Grab them reins and set Delilah on course fer Champion Ridge. We're goin' tuh see Manny!"

World Traveler

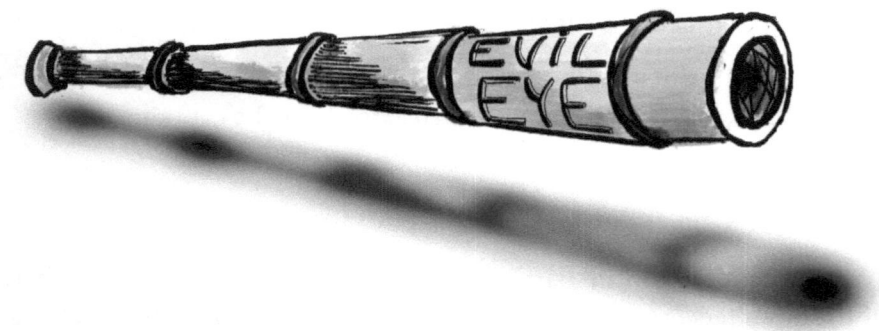

The ship flew on for what seemed like hours,

with her crew sitting at one side of the deck, Sheldon at the opposite side, each giving the other a wide berth to avoid further conflict. Sheldon did not like conflict, he liked peace. As did the three shipmates. But neither knew that about the other and so tensions lingered like the stink of the laundry pile in which Sheldon sat, being the farthest spot from the others.

Overcome by exhaustion, Sheldon couldn't resist sleep descending, the silence of the night weighing heavy on his eyes. The sandman's undeniable charm left him little choice but to put his life in the hands of fate as he drifted, finally bringing a close to this utterly unbelievable day...

Amid countless hours of deep sleep, Sheldon experienced a fleeting yet undeniably real dream about waking up in a strange bed in a strange house, faint music playing in the background, familiar but impossible to place. The dream faded just as an unknown man—a very large man with oversized eyes, even larger nose, and ears larger still, dressed in a grey-blue shirt and aged overalls—walked into the room where Sheldon lay. The man was carrying something, a tray or board. Sheldon had the feeling it was intended for him but couldn't see what it was exactly. The more he concentrated on the man, the faster the dream dissipated and soon another took its place.

It was suppertime back in his Chicago apartment and he was finishing a heaping bowl of junket after a nauseating dinner of broccoli. He didn't care for broccoli, not at all. But, oh, the junket! And Mom and Dad! Well, Mom, anyway. Of course he loved his dad, even through all the tribulations. After all, he knew—or at least he reasoned—that his dad just wanted the best for him. But did his dad actually know what *was* best for him? Taking over the family business was *not* Sheldon's idea of a fulfilling life.

I'm not meant to be a baker. I'm not meant to be a businessman. I want to create, to draw, and write. I want to see the world! Sheldon told himself in his dream. *Yes, I know*, himself answered. He slowly awoke with the words, "So do it!" echoing in his head. Recalling something about being back home, something about his father, Sheldon's thoughts lingered on being a regular disappointment to his old man. Despite that, he still felt homesick as never before. Or perhaps it was motion sickness.

Groggily, Sheldon peeled his eyes open and looked around. It was still dark, and... *Wait a minute!* Utter disbelief charged through him like an electric chill. *There's no way all of that wasn't a dream! There's no way this is real. The flying shoe thing. The three Disney dwarves...*

Walking backward through his memory, he attempted to piece together all the recent, bizarre events. *Am I actually on board a flying boot?* He shook his head and fought the urge to close his eyes and whimper, 'There's no place like home, there's no place like home!' *Darn it! I forgot to pack my ruby slippers!* he mused with a chuckle, trying to lighten his mood and make the best of his predicament. "What a world!" he mumbled, and with an, "Oh well," sat upright, yawned, stretched, resigned himself to a reality of sheer nonsense, and decided that he might just as well prepare for more adventure.

"So! What's for supper?" Sheldon barked.

Still nursing his friend's injury, the wee captain scowled at the boy and his misplaced can-do attitude. Sheldon just ignored the gloomy captain and tossed his attention overboard to the scene below.

The Chicago skyline was long gone, no building or street lights anywhere. In its place, the midnight moon lit up a decent portion of an entirely unfamiliar landscape. Feeling very much like a stranger in a strange land, he slunk down to contemplate his next move and caught sight of the large soup caldron stationed at the rear of the ship. He stole a glance at the three shipmates, assessing his odds at successfully making himself at home—as much as possible given the circumstances—by helping himself to some food.

Feeling the coast was more or less clear, he stood up, mustered his confidence, and made his way to the fine-smelling 'kitchen.' He retrieved a small wooden bowl from inside one of the slanted cupboards containing disheveled mounds of cookware and began dishing himself some soup.

The three crewmates looked on, each harboring different opinions about the boy and his gumption. The captain was wondering if the kid would try some sneaky attack, Chef Picklepots was wondering how the boy would rate his stew, and the third, the one called Tickletoes, was wondering if this kid might know how to play an instrument to complement bagpipes. The shoe sailors were in need of a new rhythm accompaniment ever since their previous bandmate—a Baroque bassist from Barcelona—had run off with a young matador during a Running of the Bulls ceremony in Pamplona (but that story is for another time).

With defensive intent, the captain made ready to stand and confront the brazen boy, but the soup man gripped his shoulder and gave him a look that said, 'I'll handle this.' Reluctantly, the captain at-eased and sat back down, much to Sheldon's relief.

Straightening himself as tall as he could, which was only about as high as Sheldon's chin, Picklepots the soup man, still holding a cloth rag to his wounded face, walked cautiously toward the boy. Through cotton and grimaces, the chef eked out the words, "It's Mulligan stew, an old recipe that's been in my family for generations."

"Smells delicious," Sheldon remarked without looking up. Picklepots glanced back at his mates, who were observing the exchange with great interest, and shrugged. The captain opened his mouth to protest when Sheldon offered, "I'm really sorry about your tooth." He glanced up and locked eyes with the soup man. "I certainly didn't mean to do that. Are you okay?"

The chef hesitated, then nodded, surprised at the boy's unexpected but much-welcomed kindness. Again, he glanced back at his friends and shrugged before returning almost entirely to his normal easy-going self.

"Ah, heck, don't worry about it none." He swung a hand at the boy as if casually tossing a baseball. "It's nuthin', happens all the time."

"Pshhhh," came an objection from one of the crew. The less grumpy one gave an approving chuckle.

"This really is some delicious supper," Sheldon gurgled as he wolfed down the glop. He had forgotten how hungry he was, given all the distractions. Slurping the last morsels then holding out the empty dish, he asked, "May I have seconds, please?"

"Hey! Whadduya know? He likes me stew! Sure thing, kid. Here, allow me." The chef neglected his injury and took the ladle, plunged it into the stew, and began scraping the bottom of the pot. "The best stuff settles down in the deep. Here, give that a go." He filled the kid's bowl. "But just so's ya know, this ain't supper. It's more like early breakfast. Dawn'll be here 'fore ya know it."

The hungry boy didn't much care what time it was. He closed his eyes to enjoy the full flavor and shoveled in a large spoonful of the lumpy gravy, filling both his stomach and his heart, not bothering to wait until his

mouth was empty before spitting out the words—along with a bit of soup—
"Soooo delicious!"

"Check out Mr. Dupree here," Tickletoes teased. "Says your soup isn't half bad! Doesn't even bother swallowin' 'fore cheerin' yer praise!"

"Dupree?" Sheldon inquired between bites.

"Oh, it's nothin'. Dupree is a friend uh ours, is all. Always talking with his mouth full uh food's'all."

Sheldon stopped chewing and swallowed with pronounced effort. "Oh. I'm sorry. I'm just really hungry. I don't know anyone by the name of Dupree. My name is—"

"Sheldon. Yes, we heard you the first time," the captain growled.

Tickletoes, who was sitting next to the captain, came to Sheldon's defense. "That there's Captain Fickleface. Don't mind 'im. He's just an ol' scruffle-grumps is all. He doesn't mean anything by it. He's just hungry is all. Hungry and angry. All the time hangry he is!"

The one called Tickletoes seemed friendly enough to Sheldon. He couldn't help but notice that this crew mate spoke in a higher, softer pitch than the others and had bright blue eyes that sparkled under long eyelashes, making Sheldon wonder if despite the beard this one might actually be a she.

Tickletoes turned to the captain. "Go on! Go get ya some glop, ya old rubber-knuckle." Then, turning back to the boy, added, "My name's Tickletoes. You can call me Tickles or Tick fer short, or Toesies if yer feelin' sweet." A loud giggle came from the soup chef and Tickles' smile broadened. "I'm the first mate of this here ship and honorary bagpiper of the Flying Festoon Brigade band."

Sheldon nodded. "It's nice to meet you all. I'm sorry about crash-landing on your... flying boat-thing."

"Her name's Delilah, and she ain't a boat, she's a boot! Take notes, boy," scolded Captain Fickleface.

Sheldon smirked. "Boy? No thanks. You can just call me Shel."
Two out of the three smiled. "So, a flying... shoe?" Shel wasn't sure he
believed the words that had just come out of his mouth. He *must* still be
dreaming.

"That's right! Delilah's the best flyin' shoe ever made. Ain't that
right gents?" Tickles didn't wait for an answer from her mates. "Well, Mr.
Shel, it's nice to make your acquaintance, I'm sure. Seein's how
introductories be in order... Your master soup man over there, his name is
Picklepots. We's call 'im Pots, but he also goes by Pickles if ya like, or just
Pick when yer short on time."

Pickles piped up on cue, "Here ya go! Heard ya say you was hungry.
So, why not have another bowl?" He handed the boy more soup. "My
name's Picklepah— Oh, Tick just said that, didn't she?" (That confirmed
it!) "Anyhoo, I'm the one n' only cook uh the Festoon. And if ya git thirsty,
I'll also be serving coffee, once the captain tells us it's safe tuh move about
the cabin, that is." Pickles laughed at Fickleface. The captain just squinted
and scowled.

"Um, I don't know about coffee, but this soup is about the best I've
ever had," replied Shel. He didn't care if he was still dreaming. He was
starving and this thick soup-stew-gumbo-gravy-glop — whatever it was —
was hitting the spot.

"You see? You see?! I've been tryin' to tell these ingrates fer years!"
exclaimed Pickles. "Me stew is the best burgoo this side uh the Qallapeck
River! Y'all take it for granted, but yuh been eatin' like spoiled kings fer
years!"

At that, they all shared a laugh as Pickles passed around a loaf of
homemade sourdough bread. Even ol' Captain Fickleface let out a little
chuckle. Sheldon took the liberty of continuing the chit-chat, considering
that the captain appeared to be warming up a tad.

"So, do I have this right, the Festoon is a flying shoe named
Delilah."

They nodded.

"And how long have you all been flying it, er, her?"

"Oh, I'd wager we been flyin' ol' Delilah now, what, prolly as many years as you been alive, kid. If not more," Tickletoes answered.

"Way more'n that!" corrected the captain, turning to Shel. "What are ya anyway? Eight? Nine?"

"Wha? I'm twelve! I'll be thirteen in a few months."

"A teenager!" scoffed Pickles.

"Uh, correction!" jousted the captain. "Pre-teen. Not a teenager yet. There's a difference, Pick."

"True," Pickles replied, "but preteens can be just as moody. It's no wonder yer so rowdy! Got all that angst and restlessness broilin' aroun' inside. Is that why yer out here travelin' the world all alone and all? Longin' for adventure, are ya? Things a bit too quiet back home, are they?"

Shel admired himself through the eyes of his shipmates for a moment. *A world traveler. An adventurer. Yes! That's me! Except...* "Quiet? No, definitely not. Home is definitely not quiet. But is that why I'm here now?" He shrugged. "I'm not sure what's going on."

Feeling a wild hair up his nose, the captain got all uppity. "Well, what's goin' on is we're headed home to Champion Ridge to see Manny because you knocked Pick's tooth clean out. That's what's goin' on!"

Shel frowned but didn't respond to Fickles' invitation to another argument. "Your home. I see. Aaand which state is that in? Are we still in Illinois?" Shel asked, trying to put the pieces together, make sense of the nonsense, which felt like trying to unscramble an omelet.

Captain Fickleface rounded on Shel, trying to sound authoritative. "What state's that in? How in the blazes should I know?! The state of Now, I suppose."

Shel was taken aback. He thought they were past all the aggressive bravado bologna. "You know I didn't do it on purpose, and I said I was sorry. Besides, I wouldn't have had to defend myself if you weren't shoving that spoon in my face."

Feeling challenged, the captain jumped to his feet.

"Oh, sit down Captain Ego Pants," Pickles jested. "I'm fine. I don't need defendin'. No more'n you do, and you don't. This here kid ain't no threat. He said he was sorry, so leave 'im be. Besides, I've had worse." He looked at Shel with a wink and a grin. "Don't mind the cappy, he's just tired s'all."

The captain exploded. "WELL, WHICH IS IT?! Am I grumpy 'cause I'm old, 'cause I'm hungry, or is it 'cause I'm tired? Huh? Which one?"

Tickle's hand shot up. "Oh, oh, pick me! Pick me!"

Pickles giggled and pointed at the bagpiper, "Yes, Tick? What's the correct answer?"

Tickles sat up straight and cleared her throat like she was about to give a speech. "Ahem, yes. The answer to Cappy's question is D, all of the above."

"Ding, ding, ding," rang Pickles. "Correct-a-mundo! We have a winner. Tell the lady what she's won, Shel." Shel just sat there while Pick and Tick laughed their heads off at his confused expression. "What's-a-matta, kid? You didn't bring any prizes with ya? Let's see whatcha got. Empty them pockets."

Shel cracked a smile and redirected the subject by looking directly at Tickletoes and inquiring, "Um, not to be rude, but I have to ask..." Pickles and Tickles continued to chuckle but looked at Shel with an invitation to ask away. "Well, it's just... I've never seen a woman who looked like you before, Miss Tickletoes."

"Oh, you mean as beautiful?" Tickles fanned out her beard. "Yes, I know. I get that a lot. Thank you."

"You're welcome?"

"He means the beard, sweetheart," piped the captain.

"Tosies is one of a kind, she is," said Pickles. "The three of us are brothers, or at least we were gunna be. But then a sister came along instead, and we love her all the more for it. Don't we?" Pickles grabbed his two siblings' beards and tugged on them affectionately.

"Ouch! Knock it off, Picks," grumbled the captain. "What Picklepots is tryin' tuh say is we three are twins. All born on the same day, at the same time, in the same place."

"Yeah," added Picklepots, "And we all have the same ma and pa too, if you can't believe that!" Tickletoes barked with laughter.

"Triplets. I see. Okay. Well..." Shel had never met such interesting people before. He'd never been on a flying shoe ride before. He'd never been so far away from home. It was all a bit overwhelming, and the Flying Boot Brigade could tell.

"It'll be all right, kid," offered Pickles with a kind smile that showed off his missing tooth. "The universe, She challenges us with just what we need. Musta been a part of ya that needed tuh get away and seek out adventure, else ya wouldn't uh landed smack in our laps." The others nodded, mumbling various agreements as they got back to their soup.

Sheldon grinned. "I suppose you're right." More mumble nods accompanied a good scraping of the last bits of soup from their bowls. "Socrates," Shel concluded.

Picklepots looked up. "What's that?"

"Oh, nothing. You just sounded like a philosopher. That's all."

Pickles chuckled. "Well, sorta comes with the territory I s'pose, flyin' 'round the cosmos 'n all in an old boot." They all had a laugh and got to wiping their dishes clean with Pickles' tasty bread before quieting down to digest both their food and all the new goings on.

"So, why were you all yelling for help?" Sheldon was the first to break the silence. The three beards looked up from their bowls, mouths stuffed with dough, eyebrows floating over their heads, all blinking in unison. "When I saw you fly over me back in Chicago."

Blank stares were had by all. The crew turned and whispered to one another. Then the captain looked sideways at Shel. "Is that where we were? Chicago?"

Shel nodded with his mouth full of bread and the twins whispered amongst themselves. Somewhat agitated by the secrecy, Shel repeated his question, "So, why were you calling for help... back at that farmhouse? Was something wrong with Delilah?"

"Wellll," answered Captain Fickleface, slowly, "I'm not certain to what farmhouse you're referrin', kid, but I 'magine that's precisely *why* we were callin' fer help. We had no idea where we were nor how we got there. It was like the Festoon was just goin' wherever she wanted."

"Which is actually quite normal for Delilah," interjected Picklepots.

"Well, okay... maybe," replied Fickles. "Sometimes she does what she wants sure 'nough. But this time she was flyin' all catawampus like; like she had a mind uh her own, and she was entirely out of it!"

"Her mind?" asked Shel.

"Yeah! It was like she had her own agenda and we weren't regarded for it one bit!" As Fickles gesticulated the details, his audience sat with eyes wide and mouths agape, like little kids being read a ghost story. Even Pickles and Tickles who had experienced the whole thing looked enthralled. "We couldn't stop 'er. She was goin' madder'n'a wet hen, she was!"

"Ain't that a typical Jezebel!" chimed Pickles.

"Careful now! She'll hear ya!" warned the captain.

"Yeah, whadduya mean by that, Pick?" asked Tickletoes.

An animated discussion ensued, which Sheldon couldn't really follow. It sounded a lot like the sort of grown-up speak he tried to avoid back home. So, taking advantage of being temporarily invisible, he helped himself to the captain's spyglass.

Mounted through one of the ship's shoelace holes was a weathered, wood-and-brass telescope with the words 'Evil Eye' engraved on it. Shel peered over the side of Delilah to examine the surroundings now that the flower of sunlight was beginning to bloom again, illuminating the strange world below. As he suspected, not a thing was recognizable. Trees were odd shapes, hillsides curled up like ocean waves or appeared to float in the air like hanging house plants. Various things moved across the surface of the land but he couldn't make out what they were: two-story tractors plowing two-story fields of corn; dinosaur-sized blackberries rolling around on dinosaur-sized thorns; giant rhinoceroses with giant lampshades on their giant horns... One thing was certain, he was no longer in Illinois.

Must be Iowa.

Delilah

"So, what makes this thingy fly, anyway? How does Delilah, um, work?"

Shel fished for answers from the boot crew, still unable to shake the feeling this was all a dream. He felt as though he were balancing precariously atop a wall that separated Crazytown from its neighbors, Fantasyland and Cuckoosville. "I just mean that I don't see any wings, like on an airplane."

The three bootaneers paused their discussion and looked around at one another as if they'd never been asked such an obvious question before.

"Well," said Picklepots, "I s'pose it's like this empty bowl here..." He picked up a bowl and placed it inside of the wash bin filled with soapy water. "If I set 'er in the water, she floats. Right?"

Shel shrugged, "Mmm-kay."

"But if I fill the bowl with water," Pickles ladled a scoop of water into the bowl, "she's gonna sink. So, all we need to do is make sure we don't fill Delilah with too much stuff and she stays afloat just fine."

Shel considered the analogy. "So, Delilah is like a dirigible then? She's filled with hot air?"

The twins broke out in raucous laughter.

"Yeah! That she is!" replied Tickles.

"Yup, she's definitely filled with hot air, ain't that right, Delilah?!" added Pickles.

Shel felt the ship rock back and forth, making him uneasy and reminding him of something. "Wait a minute! Back there, when I fell on board, the whole ship flipped upside-down, I'm pretty sure."

"Prit' near," replied Tickletoes. "Thanks for givin' us all a good shake-up!"

Pots and Tosies laughed. Fickleface did not.

"Then how in the world did everything not fall out? Especially the soup?" challenged Shel.

"Ha ha!" Pickles roared. "Kid, this ain't our first rodeo. My stew pot has a lid what stays latched when I'm not servin', mostly so's ol'

Fickleface here doesn't eat all of it when we're not lookin'. Ain't that right, Cappy?"

Fickles squinted at the chef. "Mmm. We keep most everything strapped down for just such occasions."

"Really? Strapped down? Like that loose laundry over there?" Shel cross-examined. "Please tell me those clothes are clean." The three of them looked in the direction of the laundry pile and the laundry pile seemed to stare right back at all of them.

"Well they *were* clean," replied Tickles.

"Yeah. We had everythin' folded nice and neat 'til you rocked the boat!" added the captain, wild hair a-flyin' once more.

"Yup, now it's all jumbled together: clean clothes, dirty clothes, kitchen utensils, books, walking sticks, my lucky bowling ball..."

Shel rubbed his head, "Is that what that was?"

"Nope. That was Tickletoes rappin' ya on the head with this here wooden spoon." Pickles held out a large ladle.

"Op, yeah, sorry 'bout that," said Tickles.

Shel sat for a moment rubbing his head, more from confusion than pain. He was still perplexed and concerned as to how exactly he got to where he was and what exactly was going on. Then he sunk his teeth into something. "You said you prepare for just such occasions? That's what you said, 'just such occasions', right? So I must not be the first kid you've sucked up into your spaceship!"

Fickles stared back at Shel, speechless. Before he had a chance to answer, Shel came to his own conclusion. "I knew it! How'd you do it? A giant vacuum?" The boot crew stared at Shel, utterly perplexed. Shel looked at each of them, one at a time. "What planet are you guys from? You look... pretty normal... mostly." Tales from Shel's comic books flooded his imagination and his eyes widened as he recalled the recent radio broadcast of H.G. Wells's The War of the Worlds. "I knew it! I knew it was real!" he repeated excitedly.

"Calm down, kid." The shoe captain raised a hand to steady the exuberant youth. "We're not aliens from another planet, and Delilah ain't no outer-space-mobile. She's just an old shoe what likes flyin' 'stead uh walkin'. Now, as to how you came aboard the Festoon... well, I'd hoped you'd tell us. I don't see no wings on your back, so ain't no angel nor fairy o' any kind I ever seen."

"You've seen fairies and angels?" Shel rallied.

"None like you, that's fer sure!" Pickles waved a finger at the boy and laughed.

It was becoming evident that Shel and the bearded folk were from entirely different parts of the world. Shel figured the boot crew were from someplace not unlike the worlds described in his fantasy books. He glanced at the sky to see if their heading might happen to be the second star to the right.

"What were you doin' flyin' through the air at such a late hour anyway?" demanded Fickles, changing the subject to something he felt to be more relevant.

Shel wasn't sure what to make of that question though. Usually people asked about his parents, as if he were nothing more than a lost piece of property. But these guys hadn't asked about his parents once. It was almost as if they accepted him as a stand-alone individual. For that he was grateful, perhaps more than he yet realized. But instead of discussing that, or the fact that he hadn't actually been flying through the air, for some reason he settled on, "It wasn't that late."

"Oh, I'd say it was pretty late for a young lad like you to be flyin' around in the dark and all. Never know what might be out there in the cold night sky ready to swoop you right up!" The captain grinned a mischievous grin and lobbed a mischievous brow, startling the youth.

"Wait, what?!? What do you—" Sheldon stopped short, suddenly becoming dizzy. His train of thought jumped right off the tracks and careened down a deep, dark ravine. Despite having woken from a nap not long ago, he suddenly felt the need to lie down again, his head drooping as if it were filled with thick honey, eyelids weighed down by tremendous ballasts forged from a day packed with excitement, doubt, and triumph. His triumph over doubt during his long trek on the 'sidewalk-of-fate' had been rewarded with a new sense of self-confidence, and unimaginable adventure. But his triumph in the trials aboard the flying shoe—especially since triumph was an unheard-of outcome in his deliberations with adversaries (fathers included)—had rewarded him with the best gift of all: new friendships.

The last thing Shel saw as he drifted off to sleep was a smile from none other than the boot captain himself, laying a heavy wool blanket over him. Meanwhile, off in the farthest corner of the early sky, some invisible giant reached up with her empyrean paintbrush and merrily splashed a thin blue glaze above the horizon, marking the starting line for the coming dawn.

Watch Your Step, the Game Is Afoot

The Festoon landed at Champion Ridge near midday with the sun king sitting comfortably atop his zenith throne, smiling down upon Delilah, her passengers, and all the other wondrous life in the Valley...

Sheldon was just waking from his extended slumber, feeling not disoriented or groggy for the first time in forever, but completely renewed and excited to take on whatever this new day might have in store.

"Wow! I feel terrific," he exclaimed as he jumped to his feet, stretched dramatically, and surveyed his surroundings. "Where in the world are we?!"

Tickles sat cross-legged, packing a hiking satchel. "You *oughta* feel terrific, slept most of the way here! Knocked out good and proper by Pick's gumbo I'd wager."

Grinning a gap-toothed grin, Pickles agreed. "Does the trick every time. Sneaks up on ya like a ton o' bricks, dunnit? Anyway," he stretched his arms out to present the surroundings, "*this* is Champion Valley. This is where Manny lives. I git tuh git ma tooth fixed tuday!"

Fickles smiled and nodded at his friend before putting his captain hat back on. "All right crew, Jimmy-Jack-John has called the dawn by more hours than I'd hoped. So let's get crackin' 'fore it gets too darned hot."

"Yes sir!" replied Tickles, finishing her packing.

"Hey Tick, toss a few o' them apples in my satchel, would ya? We're gunna need scrubbed teeth and fresh breath for Manny," Fickles laughed. It was clear the captain was in high spirits that morning.

They finished loading up and hit the trail, each with their own ornately carved walking stick. Shel borrowed one from Pickles, which was actually an oversized soup spoon.

The triplets whistled a spritely tune as the gang marched down a path through a wide valley surrounded by flowing hills covered in bright green clumps of billowing foliage.

"These are odd-looking bushes," observed Shel, brushing them over with his shoe.

"Whoa! Careful there," warned Fickles in hushed alarm, looking around as if someone might be watching.

Tickles chuckled. "Hey, tire-kicker, them's ain't no bushes. This here's broccoli, and uh the highest variety!"

Shel's brow furrowed. "Broccoli? Yuck! I don't like broccoli."

The three shoe pirates cracked up. "Don't like broccoli, huh?" Tickles chirped between fits of laughter. "Sure didn't seem to mind it last night!"

"What are you talking about?" Shel challenged.

"Broccoli, my boy, and Champion Valley broccoli no less, is the main ingredient in me world-famous stew," answered Picklepots. "The stew you couldn't get enough of last night, recollect?"

Shel looked shocked.

Pots laughed, "Sure 'nough! We'll be back here in a few weeks to join the rest of the province for the harvest. And it looks like it's gonna be a banner season!"

At Pickles' nod to the landscape they continued in silence, admiring the great expanse of the magnificent crop blanketing the hills and valleys as far as the eye could see. The trail on which they walked, connecting Champion Ridge to Fallshugger Ridge, cut through hillsides crowded with budding plants so bright it looked as if the entire valley were glowing. This was certainly a variety of vegetable the likes of which Shel had never seen.

"There's so much of it!" Shel broke the silence after a while, thinking of the recession-fueled food shortage back home.

"Indeed," replied Pickles. "It's a shame so much of it'll go to waste." He then added with a snobbish accent, "That is, not consumed by true connoisseurs." This comment made the others giggle. "Only a handful uh folks know the proper preparation what brings out the full flavor uh the unique Gambrine variety uh broccoli."

"Yup," added Tickletoes, "and it's a good thing, too. This place'd be right overrun and ruined if word got out of its speh-shee-ality. That's why the Gambrine protect it so fiercely." She turned to Shel. "And why YOU need to watch where yer swipin' them stompers!"

Shel smirked, looked sheepishly down at his feet, then, curiosity always on standby, inquired, "Gambrine?"

"Mmmm," nodded Fickles. "The Gambrine are the keepers of the valley. They tend tuh this crop and ensure any and all who pass here are respectful uh the plants. Very respectful."

"Ain't that the truth?! Goodness are they excellent farmers and plant 'tendants, being so low to the ground and all..." Tickle's enthusiasm dwindled and her smile faded. "But just as low is their tolerance for any behavior what might disturb or, heaven forbid, threaten their crop." She looked at Shel with high brows that dared him to doubt her. "And they have really big mouths and an awful lot of really sharp teeth." The others nodded in somber agreement. "Best to stick to the path and leave the crops alone."

"Best to stick to the path," agreed Pickles.

"Stick to the path," repeated the triplets in hushed unison, as if under a spell.

A moment of silent reverence followed before Fickles sliced through the tension. "So! Tell us more 'bout Chicago, kid. What's the thing tuh do back home? Go to the circus?"

"The circus? No, I don't really do the circus."

"Why not?!" squelched Pickles, swatting a mob of flies from his face.

"If I want to see animals I visit the zoo and that's bad enough, all caged up. I don't like them being forced to do tricks."

"Oh, I dunno," Fickles countered, "I 'magine some uh them enjoy bein' in the limelight... n'joy performin' an' doin' tricks, makin' kids smile..."

Shel shrugged. "Maybe." Then his face lit up. "I like going to baseball games!"

Tickletoes looked sideways at Shel. "Baseball? What's that?"

Shel stopped walking. "Are you serious?! You don't know what baseball is?" The three beards looked at Shel, shaking heads and shrugging shoulders. Excited, Sheldon proceeded to explain the great American pastime to the Boot Brigade as they bounced along the trail, regaling them with stories of greats like Lou Gehrig, Mel Ott, and Joe DiMaggio. Not to mention the heart-stopping moment when the Great Bambino called his shot in the '32 World Series. Sheldon was just a little bambino himself at the time, but the moment lived on for years in the streets of Chicago, especially since the Yankees trounced the Cubs that year.

"I don't normally go in for the Yanks, but my team didn't make the Series. And the Cubs are our biggest rivals, see. So we all cheered for New York that year. Plus, my dad likes 'em." Shel's shoulders bounced. "I guess they're an alright team." His favorite stories, and thus the most enthralling for his audience, were the tales of Shoeless Joe Jackson, Sheldon's all-time favorite player on his home team, the White Sox. "Poor Shoeless Joe was thrown out of baseball in 1921. A real shame. He was the greatest!"

"What's 'thrown out'?" they asked.

"It means he was kicked out, as in they no longer let him play... in the major leagues anyway."

"But why? Who no longer let him play? What happened to him?"

"Well, nothing happened *to* him. He was kicked out for throwing the World Series to the Reds. But Joe played great during that whole series. There's no way he was on the take!"

The Boot Brigade had no idea what a World Series was, nor who the Reds were, nor what the words 'throw' and 'take' meant in that context. So, the questions continued and Shel's stories flowed like the Ohio River in springtime. And despite the shoe sailors not being able to follow all the details, one thing was clear: this young Mr. Silvers was a fascinating storyteller—no doubt a result of his time in the company of his master storyteller friend, Hector the Collector. Shel also told them a bit about his school, his neighborhood, and his family, reigniting the fire of nostalgia in his heart. His dismay quickly became apparent to his new friends who were attentive listeners, very well tuned in.

"Tell ya what kid, as soon as we're done fixing Pick's tooth here," promised the captain, "we'll fly you right on back to Chicago and get you home safe to your parents. Deal?"

"Deal!" agreed Shel emphatically.

o o o o o o o

The gang walked on, following a jade-green brook that ran through spring meadows and small groves of tanglewood forest. They clambered up mossy boulders, down grassy hills, and traversed a few precarious bridges made from rope so old and overgrown it was impossible to tell where the rope stopped and forest vines took over. Eventually, they emerged into a small glen of tall, beautiful, wonderfully soft grass bordered by odd-looking, towering trees that appeared to be a crossbreed of mighty oak and dainty rose. A modest waterfall at the far end of the glen fed a crystal-clear creek running underneath a charming, thatch-roofed, stone house. The cold water kept the glen in cool climate, which was wonderfully refreshing after being out in the valley heat all day.

Shel thought the scene was utterly magical, as if plucked straight from one of his Joseph Jacobs' fairy tale books. On the opposite side of the glen from where the group stood, the groomed landscape returned to wild, demarcated by unkempt broccoli weeds growing everywhere, some as tall as trees.

"Ah, here we be!" announced Fickleface, as they approached a wooden door at the front of the house.

"This... is a dentist's office?" Shel asked skeptically. "Here? In the middle of nowhere?"

"What do you mean, *nowhere*? *We're* here aren't we? So must be somewheres," retorted Tickletoes.

"Nope, Shel," chimed Fickles, "this ain't no office. This is Manny's home." He looked back at the boy. "We shan't go to his office on Friendsday." The captain opened the door and stepped inside. "He'd be closed up right tight, and this be an emergency."

With that, the three beards slipped inside the dark house and disappeared, leaving Shel standing outside alone. "You just barge right in without knocking?" he called through the dark threshold.

Tickles stuck her head back through the doorway into the light. "Knocking what?"

Another head popped out of an adjacent window. "Come on, kid. Quit messin' 'round. Let's git to it," huffed toothless Picklepots.

Shel shrugged and slipped in through the small doorway, eyes struggling to adjust to the darkness in time to see the triplets wander off in various directions, leaving him standing at the entrance wondering what to do next.

"Hellooo?" hollered Pickles. "Anyone hooome?"

"Hello?" answered a distant voice from a dark hallway.

"Manny? 'S'thachoo?" asked Tickles.

"Who's there?" called the voice from the hall.

"It's us!" replied Fickles. "Got a tooth here needs fixin'."

"Who's us?! I'm not working today! Don'cha know what day it is?" The voice was growing louder. "It's Friendsday!"

A short scruffy man with thinning hair emerged from the hall. Other than a missing beard, he was not unlike the Boot Brigade in stature and appearance, and was most definitely a dentist if his outfit had anything to say about it.

"A day for spendin' with friends, don'cha know? And I intend to spend it with my... Fickleface? Is that you? And ol' Pots and Tosies too? Hey, hey! The gang's all here!" The dentist shouted excitedly and rocked back and forth like a bottom-weighted punching bag. He was a bundle of energy, make no mistake.

At his invitation of waving his arms about, the group huddled together like a football team, with Shel left out on the sidelines as usual.

"Well, well! Why didn't you say it was us?!" The dentist slapped the backs of his pals.

"We did. I said, 'it's us!' Didn't ya hear me?" replied Fickles, mostly to himself, knowing Manny would likely ignore him, which he did. The dentist poked his head out of the huddle and examined Shel head-to-toe.

"Say, who's this funny-lookin' fella ya got with ya?"

Shel started, "My name's—"

"Say you guys," the dentist interrupted. "I'm kinda in the middle of somethin'."

Shel scrunched his lips at being cut off, but Manny ignored that too.

"I'm actually with an important patient, back in the back. Kind of an emergency actually." He leaned toward Fickles and whispered something. Then his eyes grew large to compliment a suspiciously wide grin. Leaning back upright, he addressed the group. "Got a pretty bad toothache actually. Goin' tuh need some 'stractions I figure. Won't take but a jiff, really." At that, Manny turned and walked briskly back down the hallway, abandoning his audience to stunned silence, a hurricane leaving a flattened town in its wake.

A door creaked open and some faint words were exchanged. Then the door slammed shut and all went quiet. The visitors stood and stared at each other, speechless.

Suddenly, the entire house filled with the wailing sounds of someone in great pain. Frightened, the beards grabbed hold of one another.

"Wuh... Whudid he suh... say it was?" Pickles stuttered.

Fickles paused in disbelief at the words about to come out. "Brah... coh... smile," he spoke slowly. They all gasped, all but Shel, oblivious as to what that meant.

"Broco-what?" asked Shel casually. The beards did not respond or even look at the boy. They were all wearing expressions of astonishment and staring fixedly down the hallway in the direction of the cries. "What's a broco... smell? Sail? Snail? Whatever."

"A broco-*smile*," corrected Pickles. "S'what the locals call the Gambrine on account uh their large mouths an' typically very healthy teeth. Yuh know, from eatin' so much broccoli."

Shel gagged at the word 'broccoli'.

Pickles chuckled a smidge then continued. "Yeah, well... Wouldn't think it, because uh their ferocious look an' long sharp teeth, but Gambrine rarely eat anything except—"

BANG!

A thunderous clap echoed through the house. Not knowing what the noise was, Shel and the beards all scattered in different directions, running away from what they figured was either an intruder or a part of the house falling down.

After the ceiling stayed put, no invading army came bursting through the door, and everything returned to quiet, the guests all reunited in the main room of the house, just in time to see the tail of a brocosmile slink out the front door. The door latched closed with a loud *click* that made everyone jump, everyone but Shel. Still unaware of the grievous situation underfoot and curious about this terrifying creature of legend, he peered out of the living room window to catch a glimpse of what looked to be an oversized crocodile walking upright on its two hind legs.

Could it be?! Shel instinctively put his hand to his chest where the tooth pendant would have hung, squinting in confusion and disbelief. Without looking away he noted, "That looks like a croco—" he paused when he looked behind him to find the shoe crew had gone. Turning back to the window, he watched the crocodile thing crouch down on all fours and disappear into the broccoli bushes like smoke in a dream.

The beards slowly wandered down the hallway in search of their friend who should have come out of his operating room by now. Since he had not appeared, they expected they might find him napping or maybe on the toilet... or both.

But they didn't.

They thought perhaps he might be delayed on a long-distance call or busy balancing his financial ledger.

But he wasn't.

They wondered if maybe he'd snuck out the back for a post-op puff on a pipe.

But he hadn't.

Perhaps he'd left a note or a forwarding address?

Nope.

Perhaps his favorite holiday shirt was missing from the closet along with his tweed suitcase and passport?

Nuh-uh.

Perhaps he had—

No!

There was no other possible explanation! The evidence pointed to one clear conclusion: The brocosmile had *eaten* Manny the dentist!

As one might expect, the boot crew refused to believe that their friend was gone just like that, wiped clean off the map. So, the infallible, courageous (and oft reckless) Flying Festoon Brigade—this triumphant trio who had tickled the maleficent dragon of Grundly Grisp and somehow avoided being fried to a crisp; the three stout-hearted shoe sailors who belonged to an elite minority to have actually bumped a Glump-on-a-Rail and lived to tell the tale—those three brave and bold bootaneers decided, in the name of honor and friendship, they had no other choice but to track down that recreant reptile and get to the bottom of... the mystery of the missing dentist!

○ ○ ○ ○ ○ ○ ○

Eventually, Shel made his way to the tiny office at the end of the hall. "Where's Manny?" he asked innocently.

Pickles and Tickles shrugged. Captain Fickles turned to face the young man, placed a hand on his shoulder and advised, "Hang tight here, kid. We need tuh go check somethin'." He spoke in a serious tone but with a kind smile that reassured the boy. "Not to worry. We'll be back in no time!"

Shel squinted at the captain, not sure he understood exactly what was going on nor that he really wanted to be left behind. But as squinty as he was, the shoe crew left just the same. Before he knew it, Sheldon was alone in an empty, strange house, watching from the window as the three stout beards scuttled into the broccoli weeds in hot pursuit of the mysterious croco-broco-thingy.

Imagining

Shel woke with a jolt, startled by some loud noise. Whether a crash of something breaking, bang of something falling, or boom of something exploding, he wasn't sure. Perhaps it was something in his dream that startled him. He tried to recall what he was dreaming about but the abrupt awakening frazzled his memory. In fact, he hadn't even realized he'd fallen asleep in the first place... *In a dentist's chair?! What am I doing in a— Oh, that's right.* Again he had to remind himself of this strange reality, that he hadn't simply been dreaming of flying shoes, dwarves, and upright-walking crocodiles. There wasn't a doubt in his mind that he should be waking up in his own bed, in his own house. Instead, he was waking up in a strange dentist's office, in an even stranger cottage, in the strangest of lands. The disorientation was so profound that for a moment he thought he might be waking up from anesthesia after having a tooth pulled. *That's it! I'm actually at the dentist's in Chicago! And this has all been an anesthesia-induced dream!*

He yawned and stretched and looked around, reorienting himself with his surroundings and recalling recent events. *Nope, not a dream.*

"Those darned boot folk!" he grumbled aloud to an empty room. It felt like hours had passed since Fickleface and crew had left, and Shel was beginning to feel hungry. Ah, ha! Now he remembered everything. He'd climbed into the dentist's chair after exploring the house in search of Manny—sort of. Mostly he was searching for something to snack on. Truth was, Manny's disappearance didn't seem all that significant to him. He wasn't accustomed to life and death situations and therefore couldn't possibly believe Manny had been eaten. *I mean, come on! Eaten?! Really?!?*

He had a hunch the dentist had simply slipped out the back door, not wishing to entertain his unannounced visitors and not wishing to explain why he did not wish to entertain. Hiding from uninvited, unwanted visitors was not uncommon in Shel's world. He wouldn't have blamed anyone for trying to hide from that ornery boot captain, that's for sure.

He didn't find Manny hiding in any cupboards or cabinets or closets, however. Unfortunately, he didn't find any tasty treats either. All he found were jars of canned broccoli soaking in some sort of gelatinous brine. "No thanks!"

Shel sat, reclining in the red leather dentist chair, pondering what to do next, when all of a sudden he heard again the same jolting sound that woke him up—previously dismissed as an echo of the anesthesia.

Wiping the remains of sleep from his eyes, he rushed to the window just in time to see an enormous lumbering shadow round the house and disappear. As he leaned forward to see where the shadow went, he smacked his face against the closed window. "Ouch!" He rubbed his forehead, annoyed. Now he was definitely awake. Holding a hand over his throbbing brow, Shel attacked the multitude of locks on the back door. A knob, latch, two deadbolts, and a chain secured the door against pretty much everything by the looks (and locks) of it. After opening the door cautiously and seeing that the coast was clear, he jumped down the steps onto the stone walkway that encircled Manny's house like a moat.

At the base of the steps he froze, listening to the not-too-distant sounds of rocks crunching and tree branches snapping, sending chills up his spine. The ground vibrated under his feet while his heart vibrated in his chest. He jumped when he heard it again: the unmistakable trumpeting of an elephant!

Book I: CH. "Elephan"

Oh, how Shel adored elephants, though he'd never seen one in the wild. Back home, whenever he had the opportunity, he would go to visit Ziggy, a massive Asian elephant at the Brookfield Zoo. More often, however, he would endure a longer walk to enjoy lunch at the Lincoln Park Zoo where he would spend hours watching and talking with Duchess, another Asian elephant. Duchess was smaller than Ziggy, but in Shel's opinion, considerably sweeter. When imagining the elephants talking, he would give Ziggy a sarcastic tone on account of the elephant's obstinate behavior; behavior that was perfectly justified, Shel figured, for any animal who had to endure the confinement of a zoological institution (or any institution for that matter) would certainly feel some resentment. He felt sorry for Ziggy and Duchess. Still, he loved visiting them and imagining himself in the jungles of Asia or the plains of Africa.

But Shel was not in Asia or Africa. This place was Weirdosville, capital of Bizzaroworld. He figured he was likely to round the house to encounter an ostrich with the trunk of an elephant and legs of an armadillo. Instead, when he came around the corner in pursuit of the shadow and the noise, he did not find an elephant, nor an ostrich. There wasn't even a wee little armadillo. Like his encounter with the phantom light in the window of the old farmhouse, Shel found himself standing alone with nothing but his healthy imagination once again playing its tricks. He sighed and kicked stones from the walkway into the broccoli weeds. "Oops!"

His thoughts volleyed between the nonsensical crocodile on two legs and the elephant shadow ghost. *Maybe I'm still feeling the side effects from the anesthesia?*

He closed his eyes, put both hands to his forehead, and slowly pushed his fingernails into his scalp, dragging them across his head and gritting his teeth at the absurdity of it all. "Aaaaargh!" he complained.

"PWEEEESH!" replied a tremendous trumpeting from a terrific trunk.

"Aaaahhh!" Shel screamed and jumped into the bushes to avoid what sounded like an elephant about to pounce on him.

Sure enough! He whipped his head up to see a massive, full-grown elephant looking down at him with disturbingly large eyes, clinging unsteadily to a disturbingly small branch of an oaken-rose tree. The poor branch couldn't have been much larger in diameter than the elephant's trunk, possibly even its tail, and it was bobbing up and down, nodding like a crazy person. "Yup, yup, YUP! I'm about to crack, crack, CRACK! Better watch out, out, OUT!"

Shel scrambled to get out from under the tree, diving into a patch of broccoli bushes. From his hiding place, he risked another peek at the precariously perched pachyderm.

No! Impossible! Couldn't be! I must be imagining a giant elephant in a tree. It must be an oversized bear or some strange bird that looks like an elephant! Whatever it was, it was staring right at him with the most intense eyes Shel had ever seen.

Now would be a great time to run... away! Fast! Shel's thoughts prodded him but he was stuck. He couldn't move. *Anytime now, Sheldon!* Try as he might, he was unable to pull himself from the elephant's hypnotic stare. It was mesmerizing. It was piercing. It was oh, so creepy!

The preposterous pachyderm was sitting almost completely motionless, having achieved a sort of otherworldly zen with the tree and the unlucky twig on which he perched. Shel heard a soft voice whisper, "Heyyyyy there," and whipped his head side-to-side, looking around nervously to see who else was there with him watching this ridiculous performance.

"Up here," the whispering continued, calling the boy's attention directly to the tree.

Sheldon's mind raced. *Is there someone trapped up in the tree with that massive beast? OH, NO! The elephant is sitting on a nest like that ridiculous Horton character!* He scanned the tree for other signs of life but saw no movement, just a giant tusker who shouldn't be two inches off the ground let alone ten feet.

"Psssst. Up here! In the tree," came the voice again.

"Uh," Shel stammered. "Is there someone... up... in that... tree?" He pointed with a cautious finger. "Perhaps behind, or maybe underneath, that... very large... animal?"

"Can you see me?"

"I don't know. Can I?"

"Nope. Ya can't. 'Cause I'm hiding."

When Shel saw the elephant's mouth move, his fear was confirmed. Not only was he now seeing elephants in trees, he was seeing *talking* elephants in trees. He felt on the verge of a total mental breakdown. "Uhhhh—," he hesitated, unsure of what was coming next.

"Heyyyy!" it whispered again. "I'm up in the—"

"TREE!" Shel blurted uncontrollably. "I know!" Suddenly released from the elephant's spell, he stood up and shoved his arms out in front of him, presenting this crazy elephant in a tree *to* the crazy elephant in the tree. "You're a huge... MASSIVE... ELEPHANT... IN A TREE! Of course I can see you!" With eyes and mouth open wide, he shoved his arms out a second time and shook his head.

Feeling rather deflated, the oversized tree-dweller replied, "Oh. Well, okay then," and relaxed his statuesque posture, but not before taking one last scrutinizing look at the boy. With squinted eyes and cocked head, he gruffed, "So, you're sure you can see me then?"

Exasperated, Shel shoved his arms out a third time, feeling ready to snap like the branches which looked as if they too had just about enough of this elephant-in-a-tree business. "I have no idea how you got up there, but you'd better get down before that tree spits you out." Shel turned to go back inside Manny's house when a disturbing noise stopped him and spun him around.

What a sight! A full-grown elephant 'climbing' down out of a tree just like a monkey (actually nothing at all like a monkey). The astonishing descent was the most awkward-looking effort Shel had ever witnessed.

There was scrambling, slipping, stretching, shimmying, slumping, snorting, squealing, and even some swapping of heads for tails when the elephant flipped upside-down and it seemed he'd never get out of the woods. At one point the pachyderm made it to the lowest branch, nearly touching the ground, just a few... more... inches... He stretched his leg as far as it would go but couldn't... quite... reach. So he gave up, climbed back to the top to start over, aaannnd... *SNAP!* The branches finally gave way, dropping the elephant to the ground with an earth-shattering *THUD!*

Shel stood dumbfounded, mouth agape and eyes wide as the big bumbling beast got up, brushed himself off, stretched his sore limbs, and with one last *so there* stare, lumbered off through the bushes. With the frightening and absurd incident over with, Shel had a moment to consider what had just taken place. This was his first encounter with a real elephant in the wild and this one happened to be able to climb trees (sort of) and talk! Without thinking, letting curiosity get the better of him, Shel gave chase. He called out but the elephant ignored him in favor of nursing his injured pride, which hurt worse than his back and that hurt pretty bad. Shel picked up the pace, caught up, and began jogging alongside. "Why were you—"

"PWEEEEESH!" The elephant interrupted with a blustering blast from his prodigious proboscis. Shel crouched, covered his ears, and closed his eyes tight, trying to block out the noise. When the trumpeting stopped, he squinted at the elephant, expecting to see a raging bull ready for battle. Instead, all he saw was a large swaying elephant butt trailing through an increasingly dense patch of wild broccoli, tail-a-swooshing back and forth like a finger wagging, "Nope, nope, nope, nope..."

Unable to let it go, Shel caught up once more and resumed his interrogation. "How did you get up in that tree?"

The elephant conjured an impressively melodramatic 'what-a-ridiculous-question' sigh and executed his best 'so-glad-you're-back' eye roll. His exaggerated expressions made Shel chuckle and he wished Tick and Pick were there to share a good laugh. He quickly squashed the giggling, however, when he saw the look of irritation on the elephant's face.

"Okaaay, so you climbed."

"Well I didn't jump," retorted the elephant in a voice that matched his intimidating size.

Shel leaped back. He was already tuned in to the fact that this was a talking elephant but to hear that voice so loud and clear, and in the context of a 'conversation' was quite a shocker. "And you talk!"

The elephant stopped walking, irked by two obvious questions in a row. More than that, he was admittedly curious about Shel's apparent lack of awareness in general. He looked the boy up and down skeptically, not sure if the kid was pulling his leg or—No, the boy definitely was not pulling *his* leg. Oh, he'd know if someone were pulling *HIS* leg. He'd never put up with that nonsense! The elephant started walking again, gurgling something under his breath. "I'd stomp anyone who tried to pull on MY legs! I'd ram 'em with my thick head, take my tusks and—"

"What's that?" Sheldon cut in, unable to discern what the elephant was mumbling about.

"No, you're probably right. That *is* a bit harsh I suppose," the elephant huffed.

"Sorry? Um, I'm not following—"

"Oh, but you are, aren't you?!" the elephant halted. "You've been following me all the way from Manny's house... and a bit too closely I might add. Ever heard of personal space? Sheesh!"

"Oh. I uh... I'm sorry. I'll just—" Sheldon slowed down to put some distance between them. As he did, he accidentally trampled some broccoli bushes.

"Whoa! What do you think you're doing? Are you *trying* to get us both killed?! Hasn't anyone ever told you to stick to the path?"

Shel stopped walking and stared at the elephant, wondering what he did to get so far under the pachyderm's thick skin in such a short time. The elephant glared at the odd kid, wondering why he seemed to be unaware of some basic rules of life like don't mess with the broccoli and elephants talk. Duh.

The elephant reached his enormous trunk, wrapped it around the boy, and lifted him off the ground. Once again Shel found himself staring into those mesmerizing, basketball-sized peepers, now only inches away. "Yeahuuuup! I talk," he said matter-of-factly, then pushed Sheldon away, holding him in the air so as to get a good look at him. "You're not from around here, are you?"

Shel squirmed in the grip of the trunk, pushing out syllables between breaths, "No, I'm... from... Chi... ca... go."

The elephant's eyes remained squinty while his brows arched in surprise. "Shihhh-caaaww-goohhh, eh? You don't say." He examined Shel with curiosity. "Well, what are you doing *here*, so far from home?" Shel hesitated long enough for the elephant to come to his own conclusion. "Oh, no! You're not one of Romanov's guys, are you? Did the Falcon send you?" He scrunched his face in suspicion.

"What?" Shel replied. "Who's the Falcon? Why does everyone keep assuming I want something? Why is everyone here so paranoid?"

The elephant brought his captive up close again, right up to his eyes. "Paranoid?! Should I be paranoid about something?" His stare intensified as his grip tightened around the boy.

Shel struggled in the snake-like trunk. "Look, I don't know *who* you are, and I don't know who this Falcon fella is. I was sitting back at Manny's house, heard you romping around outside, so I went to check it out. That's all."

The elephant stared at Shel as if trying to see through him. "Hmmm." He set the youngster back on solid ground, not entirely gently. "Well, Chi-ca-go, I don't know what you're doing here but you'd best get back to Manny's place. Going to be getting dark soon and you don't want to be caught wandering through the bushes after dark." He turned and began walking away. Uneasy, Shel looked around then followed after.

"Why? Are there Gambrine around here?"

"Gambrine? Ha! No. ...I mean yes, there are Gambrine. There are Gambrine everywhere around these parts. But they won't bother you..."

"Unless you bother their crop," both spoke in unison.

The elephant stopped and looked sideways at the boy. "So you *do* know something after all." He continued walking. "No, Champion Valley is home to worse creatures than— Wait." He stopped again. "What were you doing at Manny's house anyway? I don't suppose you came all the way from Chicago because you need a dentist, even if he is the best."

"Was," Shel replied under his breath, which the big-eared beast had no trouble hearing.

"Was?"

"Yeah, I don't think that dentist will be fixing any more teeth anytime soon."

"Excuse me?!"

"He disappeared while working on a broco... smear." (Sheldon knew the name but decided to have some fun with the pachyderm.)

The elephant frowned, as much as an elephant *can* frown. "Smile. Broco-*smile*. Sheesh. What do you mean he disappeared? And his *naaame* is Manny."

"Well, *Manny* went into his office with one of those Gambrine creatures, and a little while later only the Gambrine came out."

"Well where did he go? ...Manny, not the Gambrine."

"Ummm, I don't know. Maybe the broco smelly—"

"Smile!"

Shel smiled wide, which made the elephant frown wider. "Maybe the brocosmile ate him?" he shrugged.

"Whoa! *Ate* him?!" The elephant put his face up to Shel's. "Are you nuts?! Brocosmiles don't *eat* dentists! They eat broccoli! And they like it. That's why they call 'em broco-SMILES!" The elephant shook his head. "Hang on a second. Back up."

Shel took a step backward.

"You're telling me that Manny disappeared into thin air and you were the last person to see him alive?"

Shel couldn't manage more than an 'uhhh' before the tusker continued, all the while advancing on the boy.

"You came aaalll this way from Shih-cah-gohhh, a complete stranger to the Valley—" He stopped suddenly, switching gears and prodding the boy in the chest with his trunk. "Who are you anyway?"

Shel stumbled backward and tried to answer but the elephant cut him off again with more prodding.

"Why're you here?"

Again, Shel tried to reply while tripping over rocks and catching himself in the weeds.

"How do you even know Manny?"

Fed up over being pushed around, Shel straightened himself up and stood his ground, staring perilously back at his pursuer. He didn't attempt an answer, however, knowing full well what was about to—

"Where are your parents, kid??"

And there it was, the standard inquiry. Without thinking, Shel reached into his pocket and began fumbling with the puzzle piece he'd picked up off the sidewalk, reminding himself that he was more than just his parents' baggage. *Parents*. It was the first time he'd thought about his folks in a while.

Noticing the boy's preoccupation, the elephant grew impatient. His eyes shifted wildly, head bobbing, running through all the answers the boy wasn't giving him. "Oh, forget it!" The pachyderm turned away, heading back in the direction they'd come. Sheldon shook off the nostalgia that had begun to invade him like ants on a drip of honey and sprang into action.

Emmentaler

"Hey, wait up! Where you goin'?"

"I'm going to find Manny, not that it's any of *your* business," the elephant hollered, adding quietly to himself, "I should've known something wasn't right when he didn't come out to greet me with his usual song and dance on that ol' funky guitar..."

"Manny plays guitar?" Shel intruded on the elephant's private conversation. "I like to play—"

"Whoaaa!" the tusker gasped and turned back with a look of utter surprise. "Can you... hear my thoughts?"

Shel paused. "What?"

The elephant stared with wide eyes, waiting for a better answer.

"Uhhh... noooo," Shel continued slowly. "But I can hear you when you speak."

"Oh." The pachyderm looked only slightly relieved. "Shoot! Was I talking in my sleep again?"

"What?? You're wide-a—" Shel paused and squinted at the elephant, thoroughly confused. "Noooo, you were talking in your awake."

"Oh, cacahuates!" the elephant snapped, and with his brow resuming its standard level of furrowness, he trekked on.

"Cock-a-what... ace?"

"Huh?" the elephant grunted. There was a short pause while they both tried to sort out what the other was saying. "Lemme guess, you don't speak Español?"

Shel squinted, shook his head.

The elephant sighed and mumbled, "Figures. ...I saaaiiid cacahuates. It means peanuts. I said, 'Oh, peanuts.' You know, like 'oh, nuts,' or 'oh, fiddle-farts'..." the elephant faded out, continuing to march, pretending everything was normal.

"Fiddle... farts? I get the peanuts thing. Everyone knows elephants love peanuts—"

"No! No, they don't. That's exactly the point! Ugh." The elephant turned to face the tag-along. "That's a myth my friend, like the Oracle at Delphi ... or the White Sox ever winning another World Series."

Shel cocked his head in shock. "How do you know about the White Sox?!"

The animal bypassed the baseball question. "Elephants do not like peanuts. They're terrible. Hence the use of the phrase, 'Oh, peanuts!' to describe something that's gone wrong or is just no good."

They both stared at one another for a moment, guessing at what could possibly come next.

"I love peanuts," Shel said quietly. Then he piped up, "And the White Sox are the best!" unable to think of anything else to say.

"Oh, come off it! They haven't won a series in over twenty years! Time to hang it up, don't ya think?"

"No, I don't think!"

"Clearly," smirked the elephant.

"Hey! Oh yeah? Well, you're..."

The elephant waited for it.

"You're just cacahuates!"

"Okay." The elephant rolled his eyes. "You can't use my phrases, kid. We don't know each other well enough yet."

"Oh, I think I know you well enough already," Shel grumbled.

"What was that?" The elephant swung a jumbo-sized ear in Shel's direction.

"Uh, I said... What do you know about the White Sox anyway? What do you know about Chicago??"

"Well, I know that the White Sox have been cursed since they turned into the 'Black Sox' during the 1919 World Series thanks to Shoeless Joe and his hooligan buddies."

"You take that back!" Shel's face reddened and he tightened his fists, ready to box something.

"Calm down, Joe Lewis, I'm not gonna fight you." The elephant set aside baseball to get back to the issue at hand. He prodded the kid's stomach with his trunk. "But I *do* want to know just who in the world *you* are, boy."

"Boy?"

"Oh, forget it!" The elephant turned and walked away. "I don't have time for ego trippin', kid. I have to find my friend—whom YOU lost! Whoever you are."

"Well my name is—"

"No!" The elephant interjected. "What I want to know is who you *are*, not what you're called."

"But that's my—Wait, what do you mean?"

"What do I meeeaaan? What do I mean? What I mean is how might you identify yourself if you were, I dunno, say, an explorer landing your ship on a strange island for the first time? You'd have to use more than just your name to let the locals know who you are and what you're doing there. Like, 'I'm Prince Party Pants and I've come to eat all your... coconuts'..."

"What in the world are you talking about? Party pants?" Shel whined.

"I don't know!" The elephant barked. "Good grief." He took a deep breath. "Look, what is it that you do that makes you unique, makes you special, like no one else? Maybe you can identify yourself by who you're not." Shel fidgeted with the puzzle piece in his pocket and shrugged. "Okaaay, well how would I tell you apart from a dog or a horse or... or a tree... or all the other crazy things in this world, say, if I couldn't see you, if we were pen pals across the ocean or something?"

Shel stared at the elephant, growing tired of the inquisition. "I'm not sure you and I would be pen pals."

"Oh, whatever. Look, what about... I don't know, what have you done that's worthy of honorable mention? Maybe that's the important question."

Shel's head dropped and he looked to the ground. "Nothing," he said, and the two of them fell silent.

Shel was now feeling sorry for his lack of accomplishments, his lack of identity. To top it off, he was overwhelmed by the three-course philosophical meal the elephant had placed in front of him. The elephant, meanwhile, was realizing that perhaps he'd been a tad rough with this kid who seemed a bit on the slow side. He began to think maybe he should extend a morsel of pity to the dim-witted pipsqueak. So it was that the two strangers walked on in silence for the rest of the trip back to Manny's house, giving Shel ample time to digest the rhetorical entrée. By the time they reached their destination, Shel had decided he was ready to assert himself and order up some dessert. "I am—"

"Shhhh!" The elephant smothered Shel's face in a thick, moist trunk—not the dessert the boy had in mind. The animal's eyes shifted back and forth, looking to see if anyone was around before attempting to squeeze through an open window at the back of the house.

This elephant has absolutely no concept of just how huge he is! Shel thought.

"Um, you do realize you're an elephant, right? And not a cat?"

The elephant looked back with a hardy-har-har.

"Or a bird?" Shel pitched an underhanded fastball.

The tusker mumbled something about tree-climbing-expert-somethin'-or-other and made more shushing sounds. Shel ignored him, walked around the house, and proceeded through the side door just as the elephant came crashing through the window. Shel gasped as the beast tumbled to the ground, bringing most of the wall with him.

Utterly shocked, Shel stared at this unbelievable creature. "Wow! That was... insane. You okay?!"

"Shhhh!" the elephant continued his charade as he stood up, brushed himself off, and put his trunk up to his own face this time, like a finger. He stiffened himself against the wall, and sucked in his ginormous gut.

"Uh, yeeaahh," Shel growled. "I think we've pretty much lost the element of surprise."

"Hey! That's it!" Suddenly, with the voice of a boxing match announcer, the elephant exclaimed, "Here comes... THE *ELEPHANT* OF SURPRISE!"

Shel rolled his eyes and clapped his hands to his ears as the pachyderm leaped into the hallway and charged toward the living room, trumpet on full volume.

"I said ele-MENT, not elef—oh, never mind." He watched in horror as Manny's walls became Swiss cheese, pieces of ceiling fell to the floor, and floorboards became splintered toothpicks for giants. As his rampage sputtered out, Shel slowly approached the elephant. "Well, if Manny *was* still here, he's certainly dead now."

The sarcastic comment slapped the elephant cold and he froze like a statue. Paralyzed with astonishment, Shel also stayed motionless, watching the elephant panting and steaming, trying to catch his breath, as remnants of the house continued to crash to the ground like drops of water from a leaky faucet.

Exhausted, the pachyderm sat down on what remained of Manny's couch, which held for about two seconds before collapsing through what remained of Manny's floor.

Book I: CH. XII

A final, loud crash resounded through the skeletal remains of the house. Then, all went quiet... save for the ringing in their ears.

Nine Lives

Shel muttered something about the senseless destruction of a perfectly good cottage, but the behemoth tusker wasn't paying attention. His head was bowed in sadness and surrender. As it hung—eyes studying the floor, thoughts a million miles away—something curious caught his eye. Absentmindedly, he reached out a tired trunk and grabbed hold of a gleaming white object sticking out from the rubble a few feet in front of him.

"Hey!" exclaimed Shel. "I know what that is! That's a crocodile tooth!"

"Yup. Well, brocosmile actually, and freshly pulled by the look of it. Note the root, and these markings here..." The elephant detective pointed out impressions made by dental pliers. "Brocosmiles are polyphyodonts, just like sharks ... and ele-phonts," he smiled cleverly.

Shel noted the pachyderm's play on words but also noted that it wasn't worth noting. "Poly-fi-oh-what?"

"Polyphyodont. Means we lose and re-grow our teeth over and over throughout our life. So finding an intact incisor lying around isn't all that unusual, especially here in Gambrine country. But this one didn't fall out, and it wasn't discarded naturally. This one was pulled." Quietly, the elephant continued to himself, rapping the tip of his trunk like a finger to his forehead as if trying to wake up his brain. "But why pull a perfectly good cuspid? Especially since Manny stopped working on brocosmiles years ago...," Shel looked up at him curiously and he looked the boy in the eyes, "...when one of them... ate his cat," he concluded with a raised brow.

"Ate his cat?!" Shel blurted disapprovingly.

Book I: CH. XIII

The elephont (noted) stared into the distance, adding dramatically as if narrating on stage, "Old Buddha Baggs."

"Buddha... bags?" Shel repeated.

"Yup. Good ol' Baggy Bones. That cat was so big," he looked at Shel, "and so, so fat," he chuckled, "that he looked like a small bear. But, oh, was he the most jolly and cuddly of creatures! Never rude or clawsome..." Shel sat, attentively listening to the ramble like a good friend would, even though he wasn't a good friend (yet). "Manny always talked about how he found Baggs wandering around in the snowy range of the Himalayas, on one of his many adventures abroad. Said that Baggs just climbed aboard his hot air balloon and curled up on his lap, nearly smothering him to death." The elephant chuckled softly at the vision of Manny and big, ol' Buddha together. "So, naturally, Manny brought Buddha back to the more temperate and lush climate of the Valley; much more suitable for a jolly, fat bugger like Baggs. What a place we have here!"

The elephant looked out at the fields. Shel followed the storyteller's gaze out of the room and over the landscape, and the two sat for a moment admiring the surrounding greenery, the beauty of which one would typically need a window in order to enjoy. But now, what with all the holes in the walls—some walls missing entirely—the beauty of Champion Valley could come and go with the breeze.

A shiver from the youngster caught the elephant's attention and he glanced down at the boy, wondering if he might get approval of his ramblings, and in that approval, perchance a slice of forgiveness for his destructive tantrum. "You cold?" he asked.

Shel looked up and shrugged. He might have been shivering from any number of shocking experiences as of late.

Not finding the forgiveness he was seeking, the elephant continued his story, albeit a little less enthusiastically. "With places like the Valley, who would ever want to live on a frozen mountain range? Am I right, kid?" he asked facetiously with a nudge of his trunk. "And if you ever asked him why he had chosen to live in the Himalayas in the first place, way up there at the top of the world, ol' Baggy Claws would deny it and reply, 'Now what would a cat like me be doing in a place like that?' Ha!" The elephant laughed heartily at his impression of a cat. Shel grinned, playing the attentive companion. "And then," the elephant added, pushing out words between hiccups of giggles—he was beginning to laugh so hard that tears were pooling in his eyes—"then, Baggs would drone on and on with some philosophical diatribe about finding peace within no matter where life takes you. 'Tis the Buddhist way,' he would say." And with that, the elephant burst into a roaring fit. "He was—*Haha*—the strangest cat—*Hehe*—I ever met—*Oh, Ho Ho Ho!*" His contagious laughing ensnared Shel, and before they knew it, they were hugging and swaying together in a hammock of hysteria. It was a precious moment... that didn't last long.

The pachyderm's hysterical laughing turned to hysterical crying as he navigated the labyrinth of grief, suddenly flipping from a jolly, happy elephant, rambling nonsensically about a cat, to a somber and suspicious bull. Sniffling and smearing away his tears, the elephant looked sideways at his cuddle mate with the wide-eyed, sober expression of a comedian on stage suddenly run out of jokes. A moment later, he was squinting and smirking, furrowing and frowning at the kid, maliciously flexing his talent of facial expression acrobatics and prodding the kid with a blunt yet effective tusk. "You know what? I don't trust you, newcomer!"

Shel flinched, backing away from the intruding tusk and gulping down a heaping dish of bitter cold surprise.

"I don't trust you any farther than I can throw you," the looming tusker boomed with a few more prods to the boy's ribs.

The poking was not appreciated. Shel sat upright and scowled. His emotional ramparts would not go undefended. "Well, that seems pretty reasonable to me," the boy volleyed, shoving the intrusive tusk away. "You could probably chuck me halfway across the valley—which would be entirely appropriate I'll have you know, because I happen to be a pretty trustworthy guy."

The elephant hung his ear on the snide remark and began backpedaling. "Er, what I meant was, I only trust you as far as YOU can throw ME!"

Shel stared at him, one eyebrow cocked back as if threatening to fling it.

"How about that?" the pachyderm poked, daring the boy to let the brow fly.

Shel raised the second eyebrow, increasing the threat.

Undeterred, the elephant proceeded. "Which is not at all. ...You couldn't lift me one scaly fish fin off the ground, let alone give me a toss anywheres."

Annoyed, Shel's eyelids dropped to ten percent. "Is that all? You finished?"

"Means I don't trust you."

"Yeah, I get it."

"At all."

"Okay, I get it." Shel stood up and walked away.

The elephant sent a few words following after like hitmen. "You were the last person to see Manny alive—"

"I wasn't alone!" The kid turned sharply with a timely interruption, mowing the hitmen down in their tracks.

A brief moment of silence for the fallen allowed the elephant to digest the surprise retort. Slowly, he stood up and walked towards the boy, bending his ear over him like a soggy umbrella. "Ex-kewwwz-meee?

"I said—"

"Oh, I heard what you said! What in the rippled raven's beak are you talking about?"

Shel gulped. The sight of the towering elephant reminded him of getting caught in a terrifying hailstorm while walking home from Darwin last year: the darkness that surrounded him, the cold that bit into him, the deafening hail drowning out all other sounds of the city. The chilling memory expanded in Shel's mind like ink in water, and he could see himself there again, standing alone on the sidewalk soaking in the storm. Then something in the vision changed. His fallible memory had diluted the truth about that day, the fact that he'd actually not been alone. His little sister, Meg, had been standing next to him, soaking and freezing too, trying not to panic. She was looking up at him expectantly, waiting for her big brother to lead her safely home.

Facing the looming elephant, Shel's perception of that memory shifted. He came to understand that the rain and hail had not fallen to punish him, nor was the storm sympathetic to his woes as he'd previously believed. The storm was indifferent. Yet, it meant something to each person it touched. Thinking of his kid sister, he realized he was meant to be something more than just afraid, meant to do something more than just stand there feeling sorry for himself. He took a deep breath and recalled how the piercing ice storm had filled his lungs. But this time he embraced the punch, the stabbing cold, and boldly ventured back out of the memory to face the elephant in the room.

"I came here with three others who were looking for Manny to help with a tooth problem."

The elephant loomed larger than ever, slowly spitting out the words, "What ... three ... others?"

Shel had a feeling he shouldn't say their names but proceeded nonetheless. "Um, Fickleface, Tickletoes, and—"

"Whaaaat?!" The elephant bounced backward as if on springs. "You're friends with the Flying Shoe Crew?"

"Well, no, not really. Kind of. I mean, I just met them..."

"Oh, I should've known! ...Admit it! You're buddied up with the Buoyant Boot Brigade."

"What?! No, I—"

"You're aligned with the Airborne Apostles of Ambulatory Accessories."

"Muuh... huh? What's ambew lat—?"

"You're in cahoots with the Carefree Club of—"

"Okay, enough already! No, I am not teamed up with the terrible troubadours of tittely-too. Nor have I joined forces with the jolly jamboree of jintery-joo." Shel was turning dark red.

The elephant stopped. "What are you...? No, no. That's all wrong! You can't just make up words. You have to rhyme *real* words."

"Since when? Since when are we rhyming? Who do you think you are? Dr. Seuss?!" snapped Shel.

The elephant softened his tone. "Well, I thought I was being rather clever. Who's Doctor Suits?"

"It's Doctor Soooos! And no, you weren't being clever. That's the thing with you, isn't it? You think you're so clever, that you're the big boss man, don't you? But you're not the big boss. You're just big."

Despite being lost in some strange Neverland sort of world, like one of Peter Pan's Lost Boys (Shel loved the story of The Boy Who Wouldn't Grow Up), he was definitely beginning to find his voice, and in his voice, his identity.

"You don't trust me? Well, I don't entirely trust you either, come to think of it. For all I know, *you* could be the one behind Manny's disappearance. After all, you did show up just after the whole incident."

The elephant thought about this for a moment. The boy's logic was sound, his argument not without merit. Maybe this kid wasn't as dim-witted as he'd thought. He looked down at the brocosmile tooth still wrapped in his trunk, propelling him further along the labyrinth of grief to his next stop: vengeance!

"And another thing—" Shel attempted more lecturing but the elephant cut him off, raising the tooth in the air.

"You're absolutely right, young man! This... this right here is the clue to Manny's disappearance." He pushed the tooth at Shel. "We shouldn't be fighting with each other. We should be working together, all buddy, buddy! I'm talkin' salt and lime time, man! None of this orange juice and toothpaste nonsense."

"Salt and lime? Orange juice and toothpaste?"

"Yeah, you know... how orange juice and toothpaste don't mix? Yuck! You and I, we need to be like salt and lime. We need to mob up! Find out just what in the hopscotch happened here. We need to get our friend back!"

"Well, he wasn't really *my* friend. I mean, I just met him—"

"And I know just where to start." The elephant was clearly not listening. "Come on! You and I are going to need help tracking down that caitiffrous Gambrine, and I have the perfect man for the job!"

"Kai-tifferrrr—?"

"Caitiffrous. Means cowardly... more or less. I may have just made that one up. Don't worry about it! Come on!"

"Oh-kaayyy... Hey look, I can tell you're all gung-ho about this salt and lime whatever, but I should probably just stay here and wait for the boot crew to return. I'm sure they'll be wondering—"

"Hey, I get it. That's groovy. No sweat! You can tell me all about it on the way. I'll even let you be the lime. I'm kind of an old, salty dog anyway..."

So now the elephant's a dog? Shel's eyes rolled. It was clear the big guy was going to dismiss any attempt to dissolve his new crime-fighting club.

The elephant shoved the tooth at Shel, "Here, you hold onto this," and in one swift motion, plucked the surprised boy from the ground and tossed him up onto his back. As he did, a screech rang out across the sky, the call of an eagle from somewhere beyond the clouds. The elephant looked up, startled, expecting to see a giant bird swooping down to snatch the boy, who was also looking up, squinting with a tinge of apprehension.

Struck with a sense of déjà vu, Sheldon risked the question, "There don't happen to be any boiling lakes in Champion Valley by chance?"

Seeing no threat from the eagle, the elephant started down a path that led away from Manny's house (what was left of it), in the opposite direction of where the Festoon Brigade landed ol' Delilah. Apparently their mission to find Manny was taking them deeper into this strange land.

"What's that? Boiling lakes?! Heavens no! Why? You feel like going for a dip in some hot, hot, hot springs?" The elephant chuckled. "Is that like some sort of new-age shock therapy? Ha. Kids these days."

Shel laughed uneasily. "No, just making sure." He sighed and slowly relaxed his defenses. Leaning back, he put his arms behind his head, making himself as comfortable as possible atop the elephant's leathery back. "I'm still trying to sort out where Champion Valley is exactly." Shel changed the subject. "Like, what state are we in?"

"What state? What state? The state of *Now*, little buddy, that's what." The elephant laughed.

"Noooo. I mean, where *are* we? Like what country is this? ...Or what planet more like?"

"Planet?" the elephant snort-laughed. "Thought you said you were from Chicago. Last time I checked Chicago was in Illinois, no? Arcania's not *that* far away... Least I don't think it is."

"Arcania?"

"Yeah. That's what this place is called."

"Wait. Arcania? Really?" Shel asked skeptically. "I thought it was Champion Valley?"

"It is. Champion Valley, Fallshugger Province, Gambrinstown, Kantcomplainistan... these are all places in Arcania."

"Huh... I've never heard of any of those places." Shel shrugged. He was still feeling wholly uneasy about being in a strange land, in strange company, so far from home. But putting a name to the place gave him a sense of normalcy, dare he say an inkling of familiarity. He settled into his high post on the elephant's back and quietly absorbed this new feeling as the elephant lumbered down the trail, chattering away, rattling off interesting factoids about Arcania.

Catching only a smidge of the elephant's ramblings, Shel looked skyward, marveling at the puffy, white clouds swelling in the warm, spring afternoon skies. He couldn't decide if the shapes he saw forming were visions of good times to come, or if a considerable storm was brewing. Either way, he concluded that he was ready for more adventure, surprised to discover he was actually looking forward to this Manny-finding mission with his new elephant friend—whom, he just realized, had yet to formally introduce himself.

"Say, what's your name anyway?" he interrupted his tour guide.

"Nope! No time for that now!" bellowed the elephant with renewed vigor and a quickening pace. "Best hang on up there little buddy! 'Cause I have a feeling that this, my friend, is going to be one wild ride!"

To be continued...